MOSTLY
HAPPY
ENDINGS

AN ECLECTIC COLLECTION OF
SHORT & MEDIUM-LENGTH STORIES

JIM CLEARY

ISBN: 978-1-64184-675-2

TABLE OF CONTENTS

THE
ATTORNEY

CHAPTER ONE

Maggie Sullivan possessed a rare combination of qualities. She was extremely intelligent with an obvious streak of independence, yet she seemed surprisingly vulnerable.

Maybe it was because of her size. She stood only about five-foot-three and was very slender. People often wondered if she wasn't even a bit frail. Her soft voice conveyed kindness and gentleness. Men fell in love with her instantly. They wanted to take care of her.

And Scott Sinclair was no exception. Though she'd been his legal secretary for a mere six months, he was obsessed with her.

It was the type of love and desire that could only come from familiarity. There she was every day, only a few feet away. Moving. Sitting. Talking on the phone. He loved her facial expressions, the way she sipped her coffee, and everything about her. She was perfect in his eyes. How could she not know what she was doing to him? Maybe she did.

He wanted her so badly it hurt. Not just sexually, but that, too. He longed to cherish her, to hold her when she was sad and stay up all night talking to her, to take trips with her, and to know her intimate thoughts. He wished he could marry her and spend the rest of his life making her happy. Someone that nice and that beautiful deserved as much happiness as was possible in this world and to be loved by someone who truly appreciated her. He wanted in the worst way to be that man.

But he knew he just couldn't. He was her boss. Not that the impropriety of the situation would have stopped him. After all, shouldn't true love override mere office protocols? His fear was that any come-on, no matter how subtle, might not be well received and he could lose her forever. She'd quit and he would never see her again. Besides, at age forty-six, his confidence with women was shot for many reasons. He never had felt like much of a ladies' man, even when he was younger.

So, for the time being, he would just revel in her being there every day, hearing her voice and seeing her smiling face and getting to talk to her.

"Good morning, Scott. Here's your coffee. How was your weekend?"

"It was okay. Worked mostly. Got those alimony payments to keep up with, you know. Maggie, I've told you—you really don't have to bring me coffee. That's not your job."

"I know, but I really don't mind. I'm not hung up on those kinds of things, really."

"Thanks. I do appreciate it. So how was *your* weekend?"

"Just the usual. Laundry. Went for a run. Cleaned my apartment. I'm just not ready to do much else."

"How long has it been?"

"He's been gone about a year now." Moisture appeared in her eyes. "It's still hard. I always knew when he joined up that I could end up a widow, but somehow I just didn't believe it would happen to us."

"You're young. You'll find someone."

"We'll see," she said.

Of course, you'll find someone. You're beautiful and sexy and smart. And at thirty-two, you're way too young to stay celibate the rest of your life.

"You'll know when the time is right."

"I better get back to work." She turned and walked toward her desk in the outer office.

"Wait, Maggie, there's something I wanted to mention—a compliment from one of our clients. He mentioned to me how professional you are, that you're so upbeat and always seem to see the good in people. And we both know some of the folks we represent can be a little shady."

No client said that. That's what I think about you. That's what I know about you. How can you be so perfect? You're amazing.

"That's really sweet. We do deal with some rough customers, but I believe most of them have it in them to get back on track, and you've helped many of them do it. Anyway, thanks for telling me."

"Sure. Hey, could you bring me the Grayson file?"

"No problem. I'll get it right away."

As she walked away, he looked longingly over her body from head to toe; but, as always, his thoughts came back to her face, her soft skin, her soft hair, and her infectious smile.

Sure, he wanted to make love to her, passionately and urgently, but what he fantasized about the most was taking her face in his hands, kissing her lips and hearing her soft moans. Then she would gaze into his eyes with an intensity that said she truly loved him.

He was totally bewitched by this woman. He would do anything for her. He would die for her. He had to have her. But how?

CHAPTER TWO

I t was a frigid morning. Light snow was starting to accumulate on the sidewalk as Maggie cradled her purse in her arms while digging out the key to the office door. A cold wind chilled her face. She had arrived about thirty minutes early as she did every Tuesday, so she could put things back in their proper place after the cleaning crew had been there the night before.

Once inside, she hung her heavy winter layers on the corner coat rack, but she still had the warmth of her bulky Irish knit sweater and a wool skirt. She went straight for the coffee stand and scooped dark grounds into the filter, adding one helping more than she would have preferred. Scott liked it way too strong for her tastes, but she would simply add extra creamer to make hers tolerable.

If he knew how I liked it, I bet he'd tell me to make it weaker.

With the coffee brewing, she entered the inner office of the small, two-room suite and moved items around on Scott's desk so they would be exactly the way he'd left them the night before.

Finished with the desk, she re-arranged the framed photos on the credenza behind his desk. The one earning the most prominent position was a shot of his twenty-two-year-old daughter who lived in California, far from the Midwest winters. It showed her on the beach, wearing sunglasses. There was also a pair of attached frames with individual photos of his deceased parents.

Maggie stopped to look at the pictures and wondered if there used to be a spot for his ex-wife. As she stared at the grouping, she dreamily imagined her own smiling face in a simple frame, taking up the center position. Or maybe it would be on his desk so he could see it all the time without turning around.

I can't believe I'm even fleetingly thinking anything like that. I've been widowed for less than a year.

Finally satisfied that everything was in its place, she returned to the outer office, poured herself a mug of coffee and returned to her desk near the front door. She dialed the switch on the space heater near her feet to *High* and sorted through papers to organize her morning's work.

Then she picked up a file that she had perused many times before. She liked to look at it often, like a good novel worth reading over and over. It was typical of many of Scott's cases, but to her it was a story about a good man: her boss.

A young man had walked into a small hardware store, pretended to be hiding a gun in his pants pocket and ordered the white-haired owner to empty his cash register. The robbery netted a mere $212.

Scott didn't use his legal expertise to get him off. The client had admitted he was guilty. Instead he convinced the young man to let him negotiate with the prosecuting attorney for probation and an agreement to sign-up for a restorative justice program, where he would re-pay the money he stole.

Then Scott went a step further. He convinced the store owner to hire the young man, first to work off his debt, and then to keep him on. After a few months, the owner became a father figure to the would-be criminal, who had not had any brushes with the law since.

Yes, Scott was a good man and there just weren't enough truly good men around these days, it seemed to her. Oh, she had plenty of offers to go out, some way too soon after her husband's helicopter crash. *How could they be so insensitive?*

Scott, on the other hand, would never be like that. He always treated her with respect. He was friendly, but always professional. He never even complimented her on what she was wearing.

Actually, there are days when I feel I'm wearing something especially nice. It wouldn't be so bad if he would say something, would it?

The more she thought about Scott, the more she realized she wanted to get closer to him. Maybe a dinner out some time. Or even just a lunch. *Surely lunch wouldn't be unprofessional, right?*

But she felt as if she already knew him well enough to see why that would probably never happen. He lacked confidence. He was still in pain from his wife's leaving him and he never seemed to go on a second date with any of the women he met on the Internet.

She knew she could boost his confidence in a heart-beat. When the occasion was just right, maybe when saying good-bye for a holiday weekend, it would only take a small, gentle touch on his forearm and a modest kiss on the cheek. She knew these two small gestures had never failed to get a man instantly hooked. Never.

But what if things didn't work out? I don't want to lose this job and his respect. And things are nice the way they are. We have a nice, friendly, but professional relationship. Still, if the circumstances were just right, maybe, just maybe, I could initiate a little something.

But she knew she couldn't and wouldn't.

CHAPTER THREE

Scott burst through the office door, carrying a 20x14-inch package wrapped in brown paper. Maggie smiled when she saw him, then spotted the bundle under his arm.

"What's that?"

Scott grinned. "It's for my office. It's something I've been meaning to do for a long time. Come in. I'll show you."

He set the package on his desk and tore off the paper, revealing a vivid watercolor of a log cabin. The painting showed a rustic brown cottage set against the vivid green of pine trees with the hint of a blue lake in the foreground.

"Wow. How picturesque! Where is that?"

"It's actually not far from here, maybe about a hundred miles. It's mine. A friend painted this for me years ago."

"You mean you own that beautiful place?"

"Yeah, it's been in my family for years. It's not much, really—very small, just two tiny bedrooms, a living room and a kitchen. It does have a fireplace, though. The real value, of course, is the setting—in the woods by a fairly large lake—with lots of good fishing. I just don't get many chances to get up there these days, so I thought I'd hang this where I can see it every day."

"Very nice, Scott. I'll enjoy looking at it, too. Let me get you some coffee."

"Thanks, Maggie. Looks like it's going to be another very busy day. I'm due in court this afternoon."

After hanging the picture, he sipped his coffee and stared at the case file in front of him. Maggie's soft voice caught his ear. She was on the phone with a client. He didn't need to see her to hear the sweet smile on her face. *How is she always so upbeat?*

Scott's mind began to wander. *If there was just some way we could be alone for an extended period of time, then maybe she'd fall in love with me. Maybe we'll get snowed in some night. It's been a rough winter, so that's not so far-fetched.*

No, that's silly. We're downtown and only three blocks from a nice hotel. We'd be able to make our way there and, of course, we'd stay in separate rooms. Still, they have a restaurant and we'd be forced to have dinner together. Dinner with Maggie. Nice.

He swiveled his chair around and glanced at the newly hung painting of the lakeside cabin, turned back to his desk and grabbed his coffee cup, then quickly swirled around again.

Of course. How could you not think of that, stupid? How cool would that be? A weekend with Maggie at the cabin. She sure seemed impressed by it. Who wouldn't be? It's so peaceful there, the perfect place to fall in love.

But how on earth could I—no, it's out of the question. A fantasy to forget before I drive myself crazy. Forget it.

But he didn't forget it. In fact, he didn't think about much else the rest of the day, practically sleep walking through his court appearance. The judge had even reprimanded him when he didn't answer a question quickly enough.

How romantic it would be.

For the first time, he pictured Maggie naked. Surprisingly, he had never done that. He thought she looked so amazing completely dressed. She always looked alluring no matter what she was wearing.

No, we wouldn't even make love at the cabin. I'd show her what a gentleman I am. We'd talk and talk and have this unbelievable connection. It would be true love and affection. There'd be no stopping us. We'd be linked forever after that glorious weekend.

His mind was racing. He came up with a dozen ways to get Maggie to come to the cabin, but they were all crazy and absolutely out of the question. But he couldn't shut it off. Like a tune in his head, the ideas—more like plots—kept playing over and over.

CHAPTER FOUR

Neil Muller was surprised to get the phone call. He hadn't seen Scott for nearly five years. Of course he would meet with the man who kept him out of prison and helped turn his life around.

When Scott walked through the door of the diner, Neil stood up from his booth and waved him over.

Scott thought his former client looked good. At twenty-eight, he still looked rugged and handsome. He was six-foot-two and obviously in great shape. His wavy brown hair was probably a big hit with the ladies.

If only I was in that good of shape, maybe I'd have a better shot with Maggie.

After small talk and ordering lunch, Scott got down to business.

After listening wide-eyed for about twenty minutes, Neil rubbed his hand on his chin, as if he was pulling at a non-existent beard.

"Counselor, I'm not sure what to say. You know I owe you everything—my life really, but I just don't know. This sounds crazy. Are you sure you've really thought this through? There must be some other way."

"I know it's crazy, but I'm at my wit's end. I'm a lost man. I'm so completely in love with this woman it hurts. She's turned me to mush. There's just something about her."

"Yeah, I get that, but still. Why not just go for it? What d'ya have to lose?"

"Well, everything. I have everything to lose. I'm her boss. I can't just go after her. She might quit or, worse, sue me or something."

"Now you're thinking too much like a lawyer."

"Yeah, you're right. She would never sue me. She's way too nice to do that, but she would definitely quit. She's very qualified, maybe over-qualified, so she would have no trouble landing another job. Worst of all, she might hate me. I couldn't stand that. That would kill me."

"But surely there are other great women you could meet who don't work for you."

"I've gone on a few dates lately, but nothing seems to work out. And that's not the point. If you saw Maggie, if you got to know her, you'd understand. She's special. Really special."

Neil stayed silent for several minutes, alternately staring at Scott and gazing at the ceiling. Finally he spoke.

"Okay, you know I could use the money to pay off my school loans and you know how much I'm indebted to you. I'll do it, but I have two conditions. I want the twenty grand up front and I want a letter from you explaining that this whole plan is just a game and there was never any harm intended."

"I'll certainly get you the money, but the letter—"

"I've got to have the letter—in case anything goes wrong. You should know better than anyone what would happen to me if I were ever arrested again. Everything you did for me would be down the drain. Look, I know I have a record, but I'm not a criminal. That's not who I am. You convinced me of that. This has to be a straight-forward, *legal* business transaction."

"Alright, I'll get you the letter. When can we do this? How about this weekend?"

"I guess that would work. Get me the money and the letter no later than Wednesday and we'll shoot for Friday afternoon. But if you change your mind, I won't hold you to this. You can have your money back. And that's my recommendation. Don't do this."

"Neil, you won't regret it. Everything will go fine, I promise you. I'll be forever grateful. You might be changing my life, just as you say I changed yours."

CHAPTER FIVE

Scott got to the office early Friday morning. His heart was beating faster than normal.

He went directly to the coffee station and started the morning brew. Then he sat at his desk going over and over the plan. He turned to look at the painting of the cabin several times.

His mind was racing. He thought about Maggie. He thought about the cabin. He thought about the weather. He thought about Neil and what great shape he was in. Then he looked at his stomach. No one would think of Scott as being overweight, but he had grown a bit of a belly in the last few years.

Next week, I think I'm going to join a gym. And I'll cut down on my beer drinking and sweets. I need to look good for her. Should have done that a long time ago, but things are going to be different now. A new day is about to dawn.

When Maggie came in, she was surprised to see Scott. She always made a point of getting in first. He jumped from his desk chair and poured a cup of coffee and took it to her desk as she was hanging up her coat.

"Here's your coffee, Ms. Sullivan."

"I thought I smelled that coffee aroma. I'm not used to that when I come in."

"See, you don't always have to get me coffee. I can get it for you sometimes."

"Gosh, thanks, Scott. That's nice of you. Sure is cold out there, so it's nice to start the day with a cup of hot coffee. I guess the forecast this weekend calls for bitter conditions. No snow, but wind chills near zero."

"Yikes. I didn't know that. I was thinking of heading up to my cabin and getting some chores done up there. Well, even if it's cold, it will still be beautiful."

"I'm sure it will," Maggie said. "I hope you have a nice, quiet time. I'm planning much the same this weekend, just catching up on some chores."

"So no big social plans with friends, huh?" Scott hoped his quivering voice didn't betray the nervousness he felt.

"No, definitely not. Just a quiet couple of days to myself. Are you okay? You don't seem yourself this morning."

"No, I'm fine. I just remembered, though, I've got to make a couple of calls to be sure the cabin is ready."

"Okay, I'll get to work. Thanks again for getting the coffee going this morning."

Scott looked her over. She was especially ravishing. Even though it was casual Friday, he thought her outfit was sexy as hell. She was wearing bluejeans, a grey and white striped blouse, and a burgundy blazer. As always, she made sure her professional attire never showed off her figure.

How does she always look so great, even when she's not trying to? And her flaxen hair. God, it's beautiful.

Scott closed the door to his office—something he rarely did—to make his phone calls.

Mrs. Evans was his closest neighbor at the cabin, even though she was about a mile away. She was her usual cheerful and helpful self. "Sure, I'll make a run to the store for you. The standard order?"

"That would be great. Better stock up a bit more than normal. When it gets this cold, I tend to get hungrier. In fact, why don't you buy as if for two or three people? I can always bring back any left-overs."

"Are you having guests?"

Scott chuckled. "No, Clara. I know what you're thinking. Nothing like that. And would you ask Joe if—"

"Don't worry, he already told me there's plenty of firewood. He said he'd go over and haul a bundle or two inside. And I've already cleaned the place, so you should be all set. Drive safely. Maybe we'll see you some time over the weekend."

"Well, actually, I need to work on a big case while I'm there. I may not have any time. If I miss you, I'll get you a check on my way home on Sunday afternoon. Thanks again, Clara, for helping me out so much."

"No problem. What are neighbors for?"

CHAPTER SIX

I t was almost five and Maggie was organizing her desk to close up shop when the door opened. A cold wind swept in so she wasn't surprised to see the visitor was wearing a ski mask.

She looked at the tall man. "Hi, can I help you? Bitter out there, isn't it? We're about to quit for the day. Do you have an appointment?"

The visitor coughed nervously. "I need both of you in the back office right now."

"What? Why do you need me? Why don't you take off your coat and hat and have a seat? I'll go get Mr. Sinclair."

"Listen, just get in there. Now!" He quickly flashed a hand gun and then stuffed it back into his coat pocket. "I've got a gun and I'm not afraid to use it, so get going. No, wait, lock the front door first. Hurry up."

"Please, we're just a small two-person office. There's nothing—"

"Just do it."

Maggie trembled, but locked the door and marched into Scott's office.

"Scott, there's—"

Scott, hearing the voices in the reception area, had gotten up from his desk and was heading for the door as Maggie entered, followed by the intruder.

"What the—"

"Back up. In the office, now. Both of you, over there on that couch. Sit down next to each other and be quiet."

The couch was barely large enough for two and Scott relished the fact that his and Maggie's shoulders were touching.

"What d'ya want?" Scott yelled.

"Why are you doing this?" Maggie screamed. "You must be crazy."

"Listen, ma'am, if you would both just stay calm, I'll explain."

"Oh, so we're blessed with a gentleman criminal. How nice."

"I'm not a criminal, ma'am. I'm just desperate is all and you're both going to help me. I need ten thousand dollars right away and no one's leaving here until I get it."

Scott jumped up. "There's no way. We don't keep cash here. Anyway, we certainly don't—I don't even have that much in my savings account. Why would you come here? Are you sure you're in the right place?"

"Well, you're just going to have to figure out something quick. And sit back down. Now. It's Scott, right? And you're Maggie?"

Maggie looked up in surprise. "How do you know our names?"

"I've done my homework. Besides, you both have name plates on your desks, dummy."

Maggie lowered her head and sighed. Scott jumped up again. "Don't talk to her like that. I don't care who you are. You need to treat this woman with respect." Maggie looked at Scott and smiled.

The man stared at Scott, then turned to Maggie. "I'm sorry, ma'am, I didn't mean to say that. It's just that—I'm in a terrible jam and you're the ones who are gonna help me."

Scott returned to his seat and whispered to Maggie. "Listen, just stay calm. It's going to be okay. We'll get through this."

Then he raised his voice. "So, listen, mister, we'd really like to help, but like I said, I don't have that kind of cash. Even if I—"

"Even if you what?"

"Even if I had some funds transferred, I wouldn't be able to access the money from my bank account until Monday morning at the earliest. It's Friday afternoon for God's sake."

"Monday morning, huh? Then we just might need to wait 'til then. We'll have to find some place to hole up until then. I know you have a cabin in the woods, so—"

"How do you—"

"I told you. I did my homework. Is that a picture of it right there?"

Maggie jumped up as tears streamed down her cheeks. "You can't do this. You just can't!"

"Listen, ma'am, nothing bad is going to happen to you. I promise. Now please just sit down and nobody will get hurt. Now, Mr. Attorney, get on your computer and transfer those funds."

CHAPTER SEVEN

The sun had set over the lake. A couple of small table lamps bookended the tattered couch where Scott and Maggie sat, but their faces were mainly illuminated by the roaring fire in the rustic living room.

Maggie surveyed their hostage quarters. Even under these horrible circumstances, she could appreciate the romantic ambiance of the cottage. Off the living room, there was a kitchenette with a mini-refrigerator and a stove. No oven. On the other side of the room was the only bathroom. To the rear were two tiny bedrooms. One had a queen bed, the other two single beds.

Their abductor had forced them to drive in Scott's car. Maggie had been told to sit in front. Scott drove and the man with a gun sat in back. They had to make the entire hundred-mile journey wearing handcuffs. At least they weren't metal. Maggie thought she had recognized them as something probably purchased at a sex-toy shop.

Once inside and the cabin door bolted, Scott's cuffs were taken off first and he was instructed to build a fire. When Maggie's hands were freed, she was told to fix something to eat. When chicken sandwiches, potato chips and Cokes were consumed, the threesome sat and stared at each other.

Maggie broke the ice. "So are we just going to sit here like this all weekend?"

"Well, since there's no satellite TV, I guess so. Did you want to play cards or something?"

"Very funny. How about you just let us go and we'll forget the whole thing. We won't go to the police. We promise."

Their captor rubbed the outside of his ski mask, then suddenly pulled it over his head. "This darn thing is too scratchy and with that blazing fire, it's too darn hot in here. So now you've seen my face. So what? I don't care."

Scott nodded to him without Maggie seeing. "Holy smokes. I thought I recognized your voice. Didn't I represent you about five years ago? Nate? No, it's Neil something, right?"

"Good job, counselor. It's Neil Muller. You kept me out of prison and got me into rehab after my drug conviction, but that was a long time ago and things are different now."

Maggie looked at Scott, then at Neil. "So that's how you knew our names and about this hideaway in the woods. Look, if Scott helped you before, he can do it again. You don't need to be doing this. Let us go and, like I said, we can just forget this ever happened."

"That sounds very nice, ma'am, but we've come too far to turn back now. I need the cash. I've got to have the cash."

"How about some beers?" Scott asked.

"Sorry, no booze this weekend."

"That's rich, coming from a druggie. Okay, whatever you say, Mr. Muller. I guess you're in charge."

Maggie looked into Neil's eyes. They seemed clear and sharp. He seemed intelligent. He seemed kind. He was polite. He just didn't seem like a drug addict. And he was handsome and ruggedly masculine. *Surely, we can talk him down from this.*

"That's right, I'm in charge. And don't forget, I'm the one with a gun. Alright, enough of this. It's time for bed. You two will have to share a room. I only want to keep watch on one bedroom door. I'll be right out here, so don't try anything. And once you're in there, I'm moving that table in front of the door. So don't try comin' out, 'cuz I'll hear you."

"Listen, be reasonable," Maggie said. "Let us use both bedrooms."

"Nope, I might decide to sleep in one."

"Well, at least give us the one with two beds."

"Nice try. You know that bedroom has a window and the other one doesn't. You'll just have to make do. It's not my problem."

Maggie didn't see the smile on Scott's face.

CHAPTER EIGHT

Although he squirmed to get comfortable on the air mattress on the floor, Scott was thrilled to be so close to Maggie.

"Are you okay?" Scott asked. "Are you warm enough? I can get you an extra blanket from the closet."

"I'm fine. We've got to figure out how to get out of this. This man doesn't seem that dangerous to me. If you worked with him before, surely we can talk to him and make him listen to reason."

"But we've talked to him and talked to him. It doesn't seem to matter. Like he says, he's desperate. Look, I know you're frightened. Maybe it would help if we chatted about something else for a while. Or are you too tired? Do you want to try to sleep?"

"No, I doubt if I'll be able to sleep, at least not any time soon."

He had imagined this scene many times in the last few days, and he had even rehearsed snippets of conversations he wanted to have with her. Now here he was, alone in a small room with the woman who had bewitched him for so long.

"So, Maggie, what kind of music do you like? I'm a big jazz fan myself."

"Some jazz is okay, if it's mellow, but normally it just sounds like noise to me. I prefer something with more of a melody."

"Okay well, what kinds of movies do you like? No, let me guess: romantic comedies?"

"That's what most people would expect before they really get to know me, but actually those usually bore me. Give me a good action movie, even something over the top."

"That *is* a surprise. Romance films are *my* favorites. If the characters are likeable and the story is decent, I'm a sucker for a love story. Maybe it's because my real-life relationships haven't worked out so well. So it's nice when love does conquer all, even if it's only make-believe."

Maggie sat up on the bed. "So, do you mind if I ask you something, as long as we're playing twenty questions?"

"Sure, fire away."

"I know you have a daughter who's in her twenties. Do you ever think you might want to have another child?"

"Boy, that's a tough one. I don't think so. Been there, done that. I loved it, don't get me wrong. But if I had a kid now, I'd be getting close to seventy when they got out of high school. That wouldn't seem fair to them."

"Oh, yeah sure. That makes sense. I was just wondering. I can tell you're a good father. I sometimes hear you on the phone with your daughter. Even though I'm already in my thirties, I'm still hoping to have a baby before it's too late. John didn't want to have kids and it was always a bit of a sore spot in our marriage."

"You know what? You shouldn't give up on that. And if a man really loved you, I think he would want to have children with you. Even someone my age. If I was in love with a woman, I think I'd agree anyway. Just because it would be tough doesn't mean I couldn't do it. Nothing in life is perfect. I could definitely be a father again—even at my age. Yes, I'm sure I could do it."

"I don't know, Scott, it seems to me if two people are going to bring a child into the world, they should *both* be totally committed. And both *really* want it."

"Still if—"

"We really need to—I'm sorry, I am enjoying our conversation, but I think we need to focus more on how we're going to end this. I still say we need to talk to him. I think I want to talk to him alone. I think I could reason with him."

"Maggie, no. You shouldn't be alone with him. It's too risky. He's probably high and he's got that gun. Besides, I have a plan."

"Really? You have a plan? Tell me."

"When he opens the door in the morning and before he handcuffs us again, you could distract him with small talk. Then I'll rush him. He usually keeps the gun in his pocket, so if I'm fast enough, I'll jump him before he can pull it out. Then you run for the door, get in the car and go for help."

"Scott, I don't know."

"Then I'll knock him out with the fireplace poker. If anything happens to me, at least you'd be safe."

She looked at him and smiled. "That's very noble of you, and I do appreciate it. I really do, but I think we should try my idea first. Let's give talking one more shot."

"Maggie, no."

"My mind is made up. I've got to try."

"I can see you're a very determined woman. People would be surprised that such a small woman has such grit. But if you don't succeed, then we'll try my idea, okay?"

"We'll see. Let's try to get some sleep. Good night, Scott. You're a good man. Thanks for helping me through this ordeal."

"Good night, Maggie."

Scott rolled over and snuggled under his blanket. His face flushed and his whole body shivered with excitement. *She said I'm a good man. The woman I care about—the woman I love—just said I'm a good man. This could all be working out even better than I thought.*

CHAPTER NINE

Scott and Maggie were handcuffed together on the living room couch while Neil was in the kitchen. Scott liked the feel of their bodies touching. *Nice. This is so nice. Neil is doing a great job of keeping us close. On the other hand, we haven't been able to shower. I hope I don't smell when I'm so close to her.*

"Hey, Mr. Muller, how about letting us take showers?"

"Just hold your horses and stay still. I'm going to make us all breakfast. I see your cupboards are nicely stocked. How about some pancakes?"

"Oh," Maggie said. "So not only do we have a gentleman crook, but a crook who can cook."

"I'm not a crook, ma'am, and I wish you'd quit saying that."

"You're right. I'm sorry. Let's all have some pancakes. I'd love that. I'm starved. Aren't you, Scott?"

"I am. I am."

When breakfast was ready, Neil un-cuffed his captives and they all ate in silence at the small kitchen table.

"Let me do the dishes," Maggie said.

"Alright. And, counselor, you help her, so I can keep an eye on you both at the same time."

When the dishes were washed and put away, Maggie turned to Neil. "I want to talk to you alone. Please. It's important."

"Are you sick or something?" He glanced at Scott and then looked back at Maggie. She didn't see the brief exchange.

"No, I'm not sick. I just need to talk to you alone. I'm not going to try anything. I promise."

After another questioning look at Scott, he said, "I guess it would be okay. I'll need to cuff your boss to something so he can't get away."

"I won't try to escape. I wouldn't leave Maggie alone with you just to save myself."

Maggie smiled at Scott.

Once in the bedroom, Maggie didn't waste any time. "Look, Mr. Muller—"

"Just call me Neil. You can call me Neil."

"I'd rather not. So, Mr. Muller, I can tell you're desperate, as you said. And I think you're very confused. But I don't think you're a bad person. I really don't. Look, I'm sorry I called you a criminal before. I was just angry. Scott said he helped you before and I know we could help you again. I can see there's something good in you. You're probably a really good person at heart. Please let us help you and let's end this before it goes too far. I'm worried about what might happen."

"I said I wasn't going to hurt you."

She began to sob, and with tears trickling down her face, she looked straight into his eyes. "But I don't know what Scott might do and I don't want anything to happen to him."

Neil was filled with guilt when he saw her tears and the look in her eyes. Her sincerity and pain moved him. And she was so beautiful. He hadn't been able to take his eyes off her since he'd walked into the law office.

Neil Muller had fallen under the spell of Maggie Sullivan.

"So let me get this straight. Even though I'm holding you hostage, you still want to help me? You see the good in me, even in these circumstances. Wow. Amazing. He told me that about you, but now I'm seeing it for myself. Everything he said about you is true."

Maggie jerked her head up and her tears stopped abruptly. "What? What are you talking about?"

"I can't go on. I can't do this. I've got to tell you the truth. Scott planned this whole thing. He thought if you two could spend time together, that…"

"There's no way. You're lying. He would never do something like that. He has too much intelligence and integrity to do something so sinister and stupid."

"That may be true, but he's so in love with you he'd do anything to win you over."

"I don't believe you."

Neil reached into his pocket and took out the gun. Maggie took a step back.

"Look. This isn't even a real gun. It's a toy."

Then he reached in his back pocket and took out a folded piece of paper and handed it to her. "Here, read this." Maggie recognized the law office letterhead right away.

To whom it may concern:

This is to confirm that Mr. Neil Muller is in no way guilty of any crime. His actions the weekend of January 15-17 were fulfilling a simple business arrangement with me and were done solely for the purpose of an innocent role-playing game.

This was all arranged between consenting adults. Mr. Muller is a former client of mine and is, in every way, an upstanding citizen.

The "weapon" that he used to make the adventure seem more realistic was just a toy pistol and in no way could have harmed anyone. Nor was there ever any intended threat that anyone would be harmed.

Scott Sinclair
Attorney at Law

She studied the letter and handed it back to Neil.

"So I can see that's Scott's signature alright, but let me ask you something, Mr. Muller—Neil. "Do you see *my* signature on the bottom of that page? Did you get *my* consent for this little charade?"

"No, ma'am, I didn't."

"And quit calling me 'ma'am.' It makes me feel old."

"Can I call you Maggie?" She didn't answer. "I am truly sorry. I hope you can forgive me. Maybe if I could explain why I did it, you'd understand."

"Go on."

"I owe Scott so much. He saved my life really. He kept me out of prison and personally drove me to rehab to make sure I went. Now I'm working nights and going to business school. I want to start my own business. I want to be a father someday, too, and I want to be able to be a good example. I don't want my kids to make the same mistakes I've made. Oh, I'm sorry. I didn't mean to go on and on."

"That's okay. That's quite a mouthful. I believe you *can* reach your goals. I can see your determination, but tell me why would Scott do this. I don't get it. Why didn't he just ask me out? Frankly, I've been thinking he might and hoping he would, but I knew I shouldn't be the one to start something."

"He was afraid you'd quit. I don't think I've ever seen a man so infatuated—no, in love—with a woman. And I can tell you it's not just lust. He cherishes you. In fact, that's the word he used. Cherish. And frankly, now I can see why."

Hearing those last words caused Maggie to look up at him and smile.

"Neil, I appreciate your telling me all of this. I really do, but you have to know how wrong this all is."

"I do. Of course I do. Can you forgive me?"

"Yes, I think I can. We all do stupid things. My senior year of high school, I let a boy talk me into doing cocaine one night. I could have easily become addicted, but by the grace of God, I didn't."

"That's very similar to my story. Same thing. Senior year. But I got hooked and went down a bad road. I left home and didn't talk to my parents for years. I'm still working to repair that relationship. So, Maggie—you didn't tell me if it was okay to call you Maggie."

"Yes, Neil, you can call me Maggie."

"Is that your full name?"

"No, it's Margaret, but no one calls me that. It's way too formal."

"So, Maggie, how are we going to wrap this up? Scott is going to be furious with me. He paid me a lot of money to pull this off."

Maggie stared at him. "He what?"

"But I'm giving it all back. I can't take the money. Anyway, I've broken the agreement by telling you everything."

"Don't worry, I'll handle Scott and then we can all drive home together."

"Thank you, Maggie. You're a very unique woman to be able to forgive so easily. So would it be too crazy to ask if I could call you next week? Maybe after all this blows over, I could take you out to lunch as a way to show you how sorry I am about all of this."

"Do you mean will I go on a date with a man who kidnapped me, terrorized me, and scared me half to death?" She paused and looked at him. "Maybe. Call me next week and we'll see."

She reached out and touched his forearm, then leaned up and kissed his cheek.

EPILOGUE

Scott looked up from his desk as she entered the room.

"Here's your morning coffee, Mr. Sinclair."

"Thanks."

He took a sip. It seemed a bit weak, but he didn't say anything.

As she left the room, he took a long look at her legs, licked his lower lip and sighed.

"Oh, did you find that Williams file?"

"Oh, yeah, I almost forgot. I'll bring it right in."

"Thanks, Julie."

The End

THE
PITCHER

CHAPTER ONE

U p and down. Up and down.

That doesn't just describe my career as a pitcher; it might well describe my whole life.

After six seasons in the minors, I finally made it to the majors at twenty-five. Was up for only a month before I wrenched my back and had to go on the injured list for ten days. By the time I was better, the kid who took my place was pitching great and it was back to the minors for me.

Married at twenty-one, divorced by twenty-three. Married again at thirty, divorced again by thirty-four. Oh, I had lots of girlfriends in between, but just as many breakups. No kids. Must have been me, but it doesn't matter now. At thirty-seven, I'm too old to be a dad. I love kids, but I probably wouldn't have been a very good father. Too much time on the road playing ball, chasing my dream of becoming a star and landing a contract for the big bucks.

If it sounds like I'm a negative type of guy, that's not really true. I'm just a realist, that's all. But in baseball, hope springs eternal. At least that's what they always say when Spring Training rolls around. I actually do have lots of hope that this will be my year, my summer to shine. I can see the stories now. They'll be saying how I stuck it out and made it big in my late thirties.

Plenty of pitchers are still good at my age, more so than everyday players. It's a lot harder to get the bat around on a ninety-nine-mile-an-hour fastball at my age than to throw a curve ball or a slider. Sure, it's true that many of the older pitchers are lefties and I'm a right-hander, but still, this will be my golden summer. I can feel it.

I've been with six different teams during my time in baseball, but this is my first stint with the Oakland ballclub, and they could be a contender this year. And they do need pitching, so I'm confident I'll stick with the club when Spring Training is over.

If I don't, there won't be any more trips to the minor leagues. I'll be out on my ear. I know this is my last shot. I guess that's okay. I don't think I could handle another year in the minors with all those long, boring bus rides.

Oh, I almost forgot. My name is Joe Young. Go ahead and laugh. I've heard it all before. Mighty Joe Young. I'd never heard of him before people started razzing me about it. Then I find out he's some giant movie gorilla. Oh, well. I can take it.

Then there's the obvious Cy Young references. When I was a kid, that was actually pretty cool. After

I pitched a no-hitter in high school, there was even a headline in my hometown paper that read:

JOE YOUNG, FUTURE CY YOUNG WINNER?

Those were the days. There was no way I could miss, the writers said. Well, it's a lot tougher than it looks, and I've had my share of bad luck and injuries.

But this will be my summer of glory.

CHAPTER TWO

Dawn had no last name. She didn't need one or want one in her line of work.

She'd been exchanging sex for money for fourteen years. She didn't like to call herself a prostitute, but she wasn't ashamed of the term. She saw herself as a business woman, so she preferred to call herself simply "a professional." People knew what she meant. At least the men she came in contact with did.

She wasn't ashamed of her life choice. It was her decision, after all. But it hadn't been her first choice. She didn't just have a pretty face and a fabulous body. She had a degree in accounting and had worked for a law firm for four years as the chief bookkeeper.

Life was good then. She was married to a good man and had a beautiful daughter. What turned her life upside down could be summed up in one word: alcohol. She loved her burgundy.

After losing her job, her husband, and her daughter, she was on her own and desperate. One night, while sitting on a barstool at her favorite watering hole, a man sat down on the next stool and spent a good thirty seconds looking her over.

"How much?"

Dawn jerked her head toward him. "What? You must be mistaken, mister. I'm not who you think I am. I'm just here enjoying my glass of wine and the music."

"I am so sorry, miss. I truly am. I didn't mean to offend you. You don't really look like a—you're very pretty and—well, I think I'll just shut up."

"It's okay. You're forgiven. So, tell me about yourself."

After a few more drinks and some pleasant conversation, Dawn reached into her purse to pay her tab. She saw only a five-dollar bill and winced.

She turned toward her companion. *Hey, he's good-looking and the type of guy I might have taken home anyway.*

In a barely audible voice, she said, "How about three hundred?"

"Really? I thought—okay, you've got a deal."

"Follow me," she said. "My place is nearby."

In the years that followed, she charged a whole lot more than three hundred dollars. She got herself a website and two upscale apartments, one to live in and one for work. She paid taxes on an annual income of more than $200,000.

Along the way, she went through rehab and had been sober for nearly ten years. She knew when that happened, she easily could return to accounting, but then she did the math.

Although most of her clients came from the Internet, she still occasionally liked to frequent the hot spots in the recently revitalized areas of Detroit near the stadiums where the Tigers and Lions played. Those games always brought in plenty of potential clients.

CHAPTER THREE

March in Arizona. Can't beat it. I've been to Spring Training in both Arizona and Florida and Arizona is much better. All the teams are within a few miles of each other, so no long bus rides.

There I go again complaining about bus rides. Must be an age thing.

It's a sunny day, the stands are full and it's my first actual start of the exhibition season. I'm scheduled to go three innings against the Dodgers. I'm ready.

I'd pitched single innings in a couple of earlier games and wasn't happy with my performance at all. Gave up one run in one outing and two in the other, but I feel good today.

We're getting close to breaking camp for the regular season, so this game is big for me. But the Dodgers are going with their "big guns" today. Pederson's leading off. Then Taylor, Seager and Bellinger. At least Turner's out with an injury and that's good because he always seems to have my number.

* * *

44

Well, I'm in the dugout now. Didn't make it out of the first inning. Got a couple of bad calls from the ump and ended up walking the lead-off batter. After an easy pop fly out, the next batter hit a slow grounder through the middle. I swear that thing bounced off the dirt about ten times before just getting past our second baseman.

So with two on and only one out, the Dodgers star outfielder, Cody Bellinger came to the plate. He took the first two pitches for strikes, so I was feeling confident. I'm thinking strike out, but a double play would have been even nicer.

My next pitch was a perfect slider, down and away, and Cody started to go for it, but then tried to pull his bat back. I knew it was a swing. I thought I had my strike out. I'm yelling at our catcher to appeal to the third-base umpire. He gave the safe sign. Lousy call. I walked off the mound to collect myself. I've got two strikes on him, so I'm still in the driver's seat.

I peer in to get the sign. Another slider. I shake it off. My fastball seems strong today. I was hitting ninety-two in warmups and Spring Training is the time to work on your stuff. Like most batters, he's vulnerable to anything up in the zone.

I go into my stretch and let it fly. The velocity was good, but I knew the second the ball left my hand that I didn't get it high enough. Cody's eyes widened and he let loose a vicious swing.

I knew where that ball was headed right off the bat. Sorry for the intentional pun. Just like that, I was losing, 3-0 and the rest of the inning didn't get much better. By the time my manager was heading for the mound to end my afternoon, it was 7-0.

* * *

After the game, I was called into the manager's office, but I wasn't worried. It was just one bad inning. True, it was a *very* bad inning.

"Joe, thanks for coming in."

"Hey, Skip, I know I just didn't have it today. I promise I'll mow 'em down next time."

"Joe, you've been traded to the Tigers. It's part of a five-player swap. We're getting some young prospects back."

"But it was just one bad inning."

"Has nothing to do with today. The deal's apparently been in the works for a while and just got finalized about an hour ago. But the good news is they definitely want you on the major league roster on opening day."

So it was off to my seventh team. I've only played in Detroit for a handful of games as a visitor. I'm trying to remember the dimensions of the field. I'm thinking it may not be a very pitcher-friendly park, but no place will be as good as the Oakland stadium. About the only thing I know about the city of Detroit is that my parents love Motown music. I do know one other thing, though. It's still the major leagues.

Chapter Four

D awn stared into her bathroom mirror. At thirty-five, she still had it. Her skin was smooth. Her breasts were perky. Her hair was silky, and she'd kept herself in great shape.

She had worked hard at that and hated it when people would tell her how lucky she was to be so naturally slender.

Yeah, if lucky means working out five times a week and counting every calorie I put into my body.

But the longer she gazed at herself, the more she knew her days as a professional were numbered. She'd seen plenty of the younger girls to realize the inevitable. She could land a real job, but the lifestyle would be nothing like she had now.

Sure, she put in a lot of hours, but her time was her own. She set the schedule. She was her own boss. And although she had saved up a sizeable nest egg, she would definitely miss the income.

So she tried to think of all the things she didn't like about her work. No real boyfriends. Late hours. Very limited enjoyment from sex. There were only occasional times when she really liked who she was with and would let herself go. Perhaps her main disappointment was there was no one special in her life.

Will I ever find true love? Who would want me if they found out? And I know they would. I might even feel compelled to tell them. It's better if I try to hang on for a few more years.

She put those negative thoughts out of her head. It was getting close to ten o'clock, time to go to work. It was April and the Tigers were home for a ten-game home stand.

* * *

The Royale was upscale and known for its gourmet meals and fine wine selection. Dawn had no problem being around liquor.

During the short time she attended AA meetings, she went along with the accepted lingo and would call herself a *recovering* alcoholic, but she really considered herself *recovered*, past tense. Once she made the decision to quit, she never looked back and temptation was never an issue, even when the booze was flowing all around her.

She didn't sit at barstools anymore. Those days were over. When she arrived, she asked to be seated at a corner table. She sat quietly, sipping on a Perrier and nibbled on an appetizer, and waited.

She had the look down pat: sophisticated, yet lonely. That wasn't hard to do. She *was* sophisticated and she *was* lonely.

Her clothing was always tasteful and impeccable. Tonight she was wearing a simple sleeveless black sheath dress with a V-neck. No cleavage. Her only jewelry was a silver filigree chain around her neck, holding one small diamond, matching the tiny diamond studs in her ears.

The more she refrained from appearing to be on the make, the more men seemed to find her, and the rest was easy.

It was nearly eleven. when eight men sauntered in. Dawn knew instantly they were ball players. She didn't know baseball very well, just enough to ask questions that didn't sound too ignorant.

But there was one thing about the sport she knew quite well—the finances. With the minimum annual salary for major league players now more than $500,000, she knew these young men were bursting with energy and cash to burn.

CHAPTER FIVE

We were picked to finish last in our division, but when my turn came up to pitch, we were 3-1. We'd beaten the White Sox two out of three and had taken the first game of the series against Cleveland.

It was up to me to keep our winning ways going. I shut them out the first three innings, just allowing a couple of scratch hits and a couple of walks. I took a 2-0 lead into the fourth and then was stung by more of my inevitable bad luck.

After walking the lead-off batter, I used my best pick-off move and had the runner dead to rights, but the first base umpire ruled a balk. Bad call. Then, with the runner on second, Francisco Lindor looped a single into right field, scoring the run. I had him off balance, but he reached out and barely got his bat on the ball.

I was still ahead, 2-1, with two outs and one on. Lindor stole second, but I can still get out of the inning if I can just get Carlos Santana. Okay, you can probably guess what happened. He hit one out. It was a no-doubter, so I can't blame bad luck on that one.

He hit a good pitch, a fast ball on the outside part of the plate.

So now we're down, 3-2, but I settled down and didn't give up any more runs. Had three strike-outs. I came out after five innings, still trailing. Not a terrible outing. Three earned runs in five innings. That translates to an ERA of 5.4 and that's not going to get it done, but it's just one game. Most of my pitches were working, so I'm still optimistic about the rest of the year.

The guys rallied to score four runs in the bottom of the eighth and we won the game, but it was a "no decision" for me. If it hadn't been for the team victory, my teammates probably wouldn't have been able to persuade me to join them for drinks after the game.

When I was younger, no one needed to coax me. I was often the one suggesting where we'd go. Okay, I'll admit it. We all knew that wherever we'd go, there would be plenty of good-looking young women.

They always came on to us. When we're on the road, not many of the guys, married or not, went home alone. But since we're at home, it was just a smaller group of us single guys.

Our young catcher seemed to be the one in the know. "Hey, there's this new upscale spot not far from the ballpark. We should try it. It's called The Royale. Supposed to have great food."

"Okay, I'm in," I heard myself say.

CHAPTER SIX

As predicted, within a few minutes of our arrival, there was a bevy of women around us. They seemed like girls really. They must have been in their twenties, but acted a lot younger.

None were paying particular notice of me. I don't usually get that kind of attention anymore. I'm still in great shape, but let's face it, my age is starting to show a little, especially my hairline. But that's all right. I'm not looking to get someone into bed every night. A few drinks, then a quiet night at my cozy apartment suits me just fine these days.

I was still thinking about the game and chatting with our catcher. He said next time we should go with more breaking balls. I agreed as they were getting around pretty good on my fastball.

As we talked, his eyes were wandering around the room. When he spotted a woman sitting by herself at a corner table, he poked me in the chest.

"Joe, check out that woman over there. She looks like your type. Why don't you go over and chat her up?"

"My type? What's my type?"

"Well, she's really pretty and she's all alone and she's…"

"You mean she's a little older. Is that why she's my type?"

"No, Joe, that's not what I meant. Maybe *I'll* go talk to her."

Then I took a peek and was immediately intrigued. There was something about her. She had a look of vulnerability that made you want to ask if she was okay or if she needed anything. And her hair. Light brown. Chin length. Sexy.

* * *

"So, Joe, what is it you love about baseball?"

I gazed at her with what I'm sure was a puzzled look. "Fascinating question. Seems like an obvious one, but I don't think anyone's ever asked me that before."

"Well, I love the competition and the camaraderie of my teammates—"

"Couldn't you say those things about any sport?"

She was right, and I appreciated that she had a probing mind. She wasn't going to let me get away with stock answers. I had to think for a few seconds, but once I got going, all sorts of answers popped into my head.

"Baseball is a sport where regular-size guys like me can excel. I'm only about six-feet and weigh in at about one-eighty-five. That wouldn't cut it in football or basketball.

"And, although people think of it as a team sport, in many ways it's really not. It's a series of one-on-one battles between the batter and the pitcher and each time, someone is going to succeed and someone is going to fail, and it's right there for everyone to see. There's no hiding.

"And here's another thing that makes it different. In football, for example, when the game is on the line, it's always on the shoulders of the big stars, usually the quarterback and the best receiver. Baseball doesn't work that way. Because of the way the batting rotation works, the weakest hitter on the team might be the one at the plate with two outs in the bottom of the ninth and the game on the line.

"So there. Baseball is special. At least in my mind."

"Well, Joe, you've said it all very well. It's obvious you love the game, but is there anything you *don't* like about baseball?"

What is it about this woman? She really knows how to make you think.

"Well, yeah. This has been bugging me for years, ever since I hit a batter and he missed most of the rest of the season."

"But you didn't do it on purpose, so why—"

"That's just it. I *did* do it on purpose. The other pitcher had hit one of our guys and my manager basically told me to do it. I didn't throw at his head or anything, but my fastball broke his wrist. Ever since then, I refused to throw at anyone and I've taken a lot of shit for it."

"Why?"

"Because they say it's just part of the game. But I can't buy it. That's just fake macho crap. If someone were really macho, and if they had a beef with another player, they'd confront him head-on, not throw a ninety-five-mile-an-hour fastball at a defenseless player from sixty feet away. That's just plain cowardly."

I realized I'd been rambling on and on and getting riled up, so I tried to change the subject and be a decent guy and ask about her, but it was pretty obvious she was a bit shy.

She told me she'd been an accountant, but that she'd lost her job and that she was divorced, and had an eighteen-year-old daughter. Then, the zinger. She gently put her hand on my forearm and looked into my eyes.

"Joe, this is a bit awkward, but I need to be honest with you. I'm a professional and I'd love for you to come home with me."

I wasn't sure what she meant at first, but then it dawned on me. I never paid for sex in my life. Didn't have to. I'm not bragging, but I'm just saying. But this woman had me going. I was smitten, that's for sure. She was not only great to look at, but she had a soft and gentle way about her. Not what I would have expected from an experienced call girl. And she was obviously smart.

So I said yes, but when we got to her apartment, I had second thoughts. Something didn't seem right. It was hard to pinpoint what it was. Even my pulse was quickening. How could I have these kinds of feelings about a woman like this? I wasn't seeing her as a prostitute and I was definitely more than a bit confused.

"Dawn, I think I've changed my mind."

She looked genuinely disappointed.

"Oh, I'll still pay you. That's only fair. But could we just talk for an hour or so?"

"Are you sure, Joe? I don't want to take advantage of you."

"No, really. I love talking with you. Can you put on some music? Have any Motown tunes? I know it's not our generation, but…"

She laughed. "Joe, you can't spend any time in this town and not appreciate Motown. She turned her head toward her device and said, "Play Smokey Robinson.""

After I'd told her about my dreams of landing a big contract, I admitted to her that this was probably my last chance, that I was getting old—for a ballplayer—and I was scared.

I couldn't believe how much I was opening up to this woman. Told her I didn't know what I'd do after baseball. That I didn't have a good voice for broadcasting and I didn't see coaching in my future.

"That could be okay," I said. "My life's been nothing but baseball since I was a kid. Maybe it's time I figured out something else to do. But not quite yet. I still think I've got a couple more good years. After that, though—I just don't know."

Realizing I'd been talking too much again, I stopped. "So what about you?"

"Me? I don't know, Joe. I've already told you more than I normally would tell a man."

"I guess I can understand that. You have to protect yourself. That makes sense."

She looked at me with a big smile. "Thanks for understanding, Joe. You're a very special man. I mean it."

That did it. Maybe she was just really good at making men want her, but at that point, it didn't matter. I did want her.

"So, Dawn, I may be changing my mind about our evening together."

"Oh?"

"Well, it's just that the more I talk to you, the more I want to be with you. You're gorgeous and you're so nice. And…"

"Okay, Joe, if you're sure. I don't want you to regret it later. I know I'm not what you thought when you first came over to my table."

I told her I was sure, but I really wasn't. My mind was spinning like a merry-go-round and my pulse was racing again. I was filled with desire, but part of me felt more like asking her for a second date, maybe dinner and a movie. Something more respectable for a woman this nice.

She slowly turned around. "Joe, would you unzip my dress please?"

I gently caressed the back of her neck, put my fingers on the zipper and started to pull. I only had it down an inch or so when it happened.

CHAPTER SEVEN

When I woke up, things were fuzzy. The first thing I saw was flowers. They were everywhere. Then I saw Dawn sitting just a few feet away from my bed. That's when I realized I was in the hospital.

I didn't remember a thing, but she told me what had happened. I was unzipping her dress. Well, that part I did remember. Then I yelled that something was terribly wrong. I gasped for air and said there was a tremendous pressure on my chest. Then I apparently slumped to the ground.

Dawn had called for a rescue squad, then followed on to the emergency room. By the time she got there, I was already in surgery. They said it wasn't a heart attack, just a heart "event." An artery blockage and they implanted a stent. Fairly routine, they say, but it didn't seem like a routine event to me. My idea of a routine event was a welcome dinner before the home opener.

She lied to the nurses and said she was my wife. She even signed some papers. The next morning she called someone at the Tigers and told them what happened.

All this from a woman I had known for less than five hours. And a woman who…

Several of my teammates tried to visit, but I didn't wake up and soon lots of flowers began to arrive.

"Joe, the doctor says you'll be just fine. Lots of rehab and the right kind of exercise."

"But I'm an athlete. I already get plenty of exercise. How can this happen to someone my age?"

"I don't know, Joe, but it did and we'll just have to deal with it."

Did she say "we?" Why would she say that?

It was then I realized how tired she looked and that she must have been with me for nearly fifteen hours. I told her how surprised I was to see her and how much I appreciated her sticking with me.

"They said you'll need lots of rest, so it's all decided."

"What's decided?"

"I'm going to take care of you. You're coming home with me."

"Dawn, I can't let you do that."

"Of course you can. You live by yourself and you shouldn't be all alone right now. And Joe…"

"What?"

"My name's Diane. Diane Lincoln."

I stuck out my hand and she shook it. "It's nice to meet you, Diane."

"Pleased to meet you, too, Joe Young."

* * *

THREE DAYS LATER

The first thing I remember when we got to her place was everything was different. Although things were still a bit fuzzy, this didn't look at all like where we were a few nights ago.

"This is where I live, Joe. The other place is where I work. There's not a full kitchen there, nor any food. This is where you need to be. I never bring anyone here. You're the first man who's ever set foot in here."

I was still on bed rest, but was sitting up. She brought me a bowl of soup and some delicious dinner rolls. They seemed homemade.

"How do you find time to bake?"

She giggled. "Joe, I'm not working *all* the time."

What happened next was the real shocker. She leaned over the bedside and planted, a long, passionate kiss on my lips.

"Wow, Dawn. I mean Diane. Are you kidding me? I think I'm getting better already. But I've got a ways to go, I know. So, can we do that again?"

Over the next few days, we did kiss, a lot. Kisses and soup. Hugs and pasta. Touching and long conversations. It was like a dream. But I knew it had to end. That's when the elephant in the room finally came up: my career.

She was so encouraging. "They say you'll have a full recovery, but the bad news is you'll be out for the season. Still, you'll have a year to get back in shape and try again next year."

But I knew that wasn't going to happen. Sure, I could have busted my butt and gone for another comeback next spring, but somewhere down deep, I knew it was over. It was time to move on. There had to be life after baseball.

It turned out that wasn't the only elephant in the room. What about her, us? She had said "we" and that stuck in my mind. I'd been thinking about it from the start, but doubted she had. Yet here she was, going so far out of her way to take care of me.

She'd probably had other customers fall in love with her, but she'd said I was the first guy she'd ever brought to her real apartment. That must count for something. And she kept saying how we were both in the same boat in a way—both nearing the retirement age for athletes.

So I just came right out and said it. "I don't want this to end. I want us to be together."

"Joe, you can't mean that." Her eyes looked sad, like she knew it would never really happen.

"I do mean it. I know what you're thinking, but I don't care. The past is the past. We're both at a cross-roads. Let's start over. Together."

"You say that now, but what about years from now? You'll be thinking of all the men I've been with and it might tear you apart and you'll end up hating me."

"I would never hate you and besides, what about all the women I've been with? No need to do any counting. Let's just say we're even."

I didn't get much sleep that night, even though I needed it. She was all I could think about. And I began to have second thoughts. What if she was right? Could I really forget about her past?

Then I realized something. I was no longer worried about what I'd do when I couldn't pitch anymore. Suddenly, saying goodbye to my lifetime Earned Run Average of 7.63 didn't seem like such a bad idea. Even though I didn't know what the future held, I was looking forward to it. And there was only one possible reason for this change of thinking: Diane.

I'd made plenty of money in my various stints in the majors and if I could be with Diane, the next chapter in my life didn't seem so scary. In fact, I was excited to get started.

And if there had still been any doubts, they would have vanished the next morning when she brought me breakfast in bed and looked into my eyes. Wow! What a look of love. I had never felt this way about a woman before, and I hadn't even been to bed with her, although I sure wanted to. It was an incredible feeling.

After I'd finished breakfast, she sat there silently staring at me, so I spoke up. I'd been thinking of asking her this all morning.

"So, Diane, are you going to have to work tonight?"

She looked at me and grinned. "You think you're pretty clever, don't you? I know what you're getting at. No, Joe. The answer is no. I've already canceled my appointments. I'm staying with you tonight."

"So does this mean what I think it means?"

"We'll see."

I tried to win her over with big dreams. "Why don't we take a trip together? How about a cruise in the Caribbean? We've both got plenty of money. We could get to know each other, and plan our future. Then we could move to a new city where people don't know us and plan new careers for ourselves. Hey, maybe we could start a business together and—"

"Whoa, slow down, Joe. I love your enthusiasm, but we hardly know each other. You think you know the worst thing about me, but you really don't."

That's when she told me about her days as a drunk, her divorce, and the anguish and guilt she felt about her daughter.

"She's always lived with her dad and I've only seen her a handful of times over the years and it's always very strained. She's in college now, an adult really. I know I only have myself to blame, but I just wish I could find a way to reconnect with her."

Feeling a rush of confidence and optimism, I told her that, since we'd both be starting over, we'd figure out a way to bring her daughter into our new life.

"Joe, I don't know. Let's just take one step at a time."

"Okay, we'll take one step at a time," I said. "Let's go on a cruise. Could you take at least a month off?"

When she leaned in and gave me a long, passionate kiss, I had my answer.

EPILOGUE

ONE YEAR LATER IN MAUI

The young woman entered the office located in a small strip mall. She fixed herself a cup of coffee and gazed out the window. Across the busy street was a beautiful sandy beach and the Pacific Ocean. Her thoughts were interrupted by the ringing phone.

"D&J Island Tours. This is Lisa. Can I help you?"

"Good morning, Lisa."

"Oh, hi, Joe…No, Mom's not here yet. Will you be in soon? Wait, she's just walking in the door now. Here you go. See you in a little bit."

"Diane, I forgot to tell you. A guy's coming in this morning to book a tour for his extended family. They'll be flying in from Japan on Friday. About thirty people. It'll be a big chunk of business for us. I should be there in time, but just in case…"

After the phone call, Diane smiled at Lisa. "It's another perfect morning in paradise, especially with you here, hon. I love you."

"I know you do, Mom. I love you, too."

* * *

"Well, I think we're all set Mr. Hamada. I know you and your family will have a great time," Joe said. "This is our deluxe, all-day tour. It starts with a sunrise trip to the Haleakala Crater. It includes lunch and a whole lot more. I know you'll love it. By the way, I forgot to ask how you heard about us."

"I saw your ad on the Internet, but I have to confess I recognized your name. I'm a big baseball fan."

"Really? You must be a *really* big fan if you've heard of a journeyman pitcher like me."

"Besides, when I was on your website, I saw the photos of you and your wife. I like dealing with family-owned businesses. You and Diane seem like such a nice couple. How did you two meet anyway?"

Before answering, Joe looked at Diane and she grinned. "Ah, well, that's a long story. Maybe another time. The main thing is we found each other and we couldn't be happier that we did."

The End

THE HIKER

CHAPTER ONE

Sarah Jenkins trudged up the familiar steep trail through a thick forest, breathing in the ambrosial pine fragrance. Arriving at an expansive clearing, she stopped and leaned on her trekking pole.

The open meadow was filled with wildflowers and tall grasses. Towering above were snow-capped peaks rising twelve thousand feet into a vivid blue sky, forming a horseshoe around the valley she was entering.

She came here for the view. Today, though, Sarah's appreciation of its awesome grandeur was marred by thoughts of her boyfriend Ryan and their less-than-fulfilling relationship.

She shook off those confusing feelings, however, and continued on. Her blond ponytail, tucked through the opening in her bright turquoise baseball cap, bobbed in rhythm to her steady, deliberate uphill pace. The tan, mid-length shorts she wore showed off long, shapely legs. For a woman of thirty-two, Sarah retained the beauty and vitality of her teen years.

Waitressing in the nearby mountain resort town gave her enough income to survive and plenty of time to pursue her passion of hiking three or four times a week in what she often said were *her* amazing mountains.

Sarah resented how some of her friends considered her obsessed. She wasn't. She was passionate. To her it was a simple matter of spending time doing what she loved. She often wished Ryan shared her passion, but he did not. So she hiked alone.

Ryan's lack of interest would be okay with her if they shared other activities or interests. She'd been living with him for three months and she did care for him. He was smart enough to talk on any subject, yet they never engaged in any meaningful conversations. Their relationship hadn't progressed past small talk and great sex.

She'd had lots of boyfriends in the last few years, but she knew none of them was the one she would end up with. And that included Ryan, so maybe it *was* time to break up.

She wanted to find true love and have a family. Her friends told her that, with her cheerful disposition, along with her kind and patient demeanor, she'd make a great mom.

With a college degree in journalism, she knew she could move to a bigger city, make more money, and have a more stimulating social life, including a much wider pool of men.

But she wasn't ready to give up on having both, at least not just yet, so relocating was out of the question. The lure of the mountains was still too strong and today was another inspiring day in paradise. So up the trail she sailed.

CHAPTER TWO

She was nearing the turn-around point of her fourteen-mile journey and hadn't seen another human for at least two hours. The lower sections of the trail had been teeming with tourists and would-be hikers, families with kids, and folks in tennis shoes and sandals with little or no water. But now she was alone and thinking about lunch as she neared her destination: a stunning open meadow containing three small lakes.

Reaching the shoreline of the closest pond, Sarah found a rock flat enough to serve as a picnic bench. The air was cooler at this altitude, the views breathtaking and the solitude made this spot seem almost spiritual.

She shrugged off her backpack and grabbed her peanut butter and jelly sandwich, an apple and an energy bar. After eating, she took out her camera and snapped a series of shots, trying to capture the awesome scene, but she knew that even her best photos could never do justice to what she was experiencing.

Wanting to linger a while longer, she propped her backpack against a rock and used it as a pillow. If she could stop wondering what to do about Ryan, she might doze off for a few peaceful minutes.

After relaxing for half an hour, she looked around to see if there were any other hikers approaching. Seeing no one, she decided to take a quick dip in the lake. The chances of anyone coming along were remote, and if they did, she didn't care. She wasn't an exhibitionist, but she wasn't shy either. If someone did happen along, she'd quickly dress, apologize, and head on down the trail.

Sarah pulled off her hiking boots and undressed, setting her clothes on a nearby rock. Now naked, she looked around one more time. Still seeing no one, she eased herself over a boulder and slid into the water.

She knew it would be icy, but she didn't mind. It would be refreshing and she figured her swim would be brief.

"Yikes. That's cold alright." She splashed around for only a few minutes, making sure to keep her hair dry. When climbing out of the water, she grabbed onto a boulder to pull herself out, but lost her grip.

As she fell backwards, she tried to regain her balance by jamming her right foot into the ground. She yelped in pain as her whole body tumbled backwards into the lake.

Now sitting in the shallow water, she grabbed her ankle, realizing right away that one of three things had just happened and none of them were good. Either it was broken, sprained or, with a little bit of luck, maybe only twisted. Regardless, it was going to be a long, painful journey back to the trailhead. Seven long miles. No cell signal. And no help in sight.

CHAPTER THREE

After struggling to hoist herself onto the shore, her first step on the damaged ankle brought excruciating pain. She hopped to her clothes and dressed while sitting on a rock. After lacing up her left boot, she tried putting on the right one, but the swelling wouldn't allow it.

Sarah was not prone to panic, but she did begin to worry a bit. Limping in pain for seven miles would be hard enough, but negotiating the rocky trail with no boot was unthinkable. Somehow, she had to get that boot on her injured foot.

She dragged herself back to the water, took off her sock and put her foot in the cold water, hoping to reduce the inflammation. After soaking for ten minutes, the knot wasn't any smaller, but it had become numb. She loosened the laces and tried again to force the boot past her ankle. She cried out as it slid on. She left the laces slackened.

Using her pole as a crutch, Sarah walked the first few steps, putting as little weight on her injured foot as possible. The throbbing was intense, and she sat down on the first nearby rock to re-assess her predicament.

Tears threatened, but she wasn't about to cry. All hikers understood that despite the beautiful surroundings and the nicely maintained trail, when you're this far into the wilderness, you're on your own. At this agonizingly slow pace, the normally three-hour trek could take eight hours or more. And, even though it was mid-summer, she realized it would be well after dark by the time she reached her car.

As she pulled herself off the rock to resume her painful journey, she heard the crunching of boots on the trail. *Thank God. I'm rescued.* She sat back down and waited, listening to the sound getting closer. Then it stopped and there was silence.

"Hey, is someone there? "Help! I need help."

She stared at the trail, waiting, listening, hoping. Finally, she heard movement again and a man rounded the bend into view.

Sarah prided herself on being independent. She didn't need a man to make it—in life or on the trail. But right now she would welcome help from anyone—a man, woman, or even a child or an old lady.

She cradled her injured foot with one arm so she could twist her body toward him. *Okay, it's not a small child or an old lady. It's a man and he looks young enough and strong enough to help me get home. Good.*

"Are you okay? Was that you calling for help?"

"Yep, that was me. Turned my ankle. I'm pretty sure it's sprained and we're a long ways up here."

"Yeah we are." He leaned down and offered a handshake. "I'm Joel Rosen." Sarah noticed it was a full, firm handshake. She always hated how so many men offered a limp hand or grabbed hers as if they were going to kiss it.

"Joe, I'm Sarah."

"No, it's Joel, not Joe."

"Sorry."

"Don't worry. A lot of people make that mistake. Would you like me to take a look at your ankle?"

"No, it was too painful to pull my boot on. I don't want to have to go through that again."

"Understood. I've had a sprain before. They're tough. Worse than a break, really. It doesn't look like we have too many options. I suggest you use your hiking pole on your good side and lean on me on the injured side. Don't worry, we'll get you down."

"You're a life saver. I can't tell you how much I appreciate this."

"Do you always hike alone?"

"Not always, but often. I've been hiking these mountains for years and I've never had anything like this happen before. Shall we get started?"

"Before we go, do you mind if I stop a minute to take in this amazing view?"

"Of course. I'm so sorry. You just got here and instead of enjoying some time in this beautiful spot, you're having to deal with me."

"It's okay, really. I don't mind. But this is an amazing sight."

"Well, if you'd gotten here a few minutes earlier, the view would have included a nude woman swimming in that lake."

Joel laughed. "Really?"

"Yeah, I do that sometimes."

He quickly scanned her body. "Well, it's just my luck. If I hadn't had that second cup of coffee this morning..."

With a smile still playing at the corners of his mouth, Joel turned in every direction to absorb the beauty of the vistas and Sarah took advantage of the lull to look him over.

He was about six feet, with broad shoulders and thickset, but not overweight. He wore black-rimmed glasses; his bushy, curly hair was salt and pepper. About forty, she guessed.

After some deep breaths, Joel leaned down to pick up her backpack. "Your pack is small. I think I can stuff it inside mine."

"No, you don't need to do that. I can carry it."

"It's no problem. We need you to have as little weight on that ankle as possible."

"Thank you."

"Okay, let's do it. We'll take it slow. Just one step at a time."

"Good plan, Joel. I tried two steps at a time once, but it just didn't work very well."

He laughed. "You're quite the livewire, aren't you?"

"I've been called worse."

He helped her to her feet and she eased her arm around his shoulder.

"Jenkins."

"What?"

"Sarah Jenkins. My last name is Jenkins."

"Okay, Sarah Jenkins. Here we go."

CHAPTER FOUR

Sarah winced with every step, but Joel's constant blitzing her with questions helped distract her. She happily spilled everything about her life, including Ryan. After an hour, they spotted a couple of good sittin' rocks by a stream and took a break.

"I don't usually babble on about myself like this, but you're so easy to talk to, and I'm grateful you're interested."

'I *am* interested and you've got fascinating stories."

I lucked out finding such a nice guy to help me. He's not bad looking either. And I'm telling this guy stuff like I've known him for years. Talking to Ryan is never like this. This is what it's supposed to be like.

"So what about you? What's your story?"

"I'm from Minnesota, here on vacation, and I'm an investment banker."

"You mean you're a stockbroker?"

"Investment banker."

"So, you buy and sell stocks and bonds for your clients, right?"

"Yeah."

"So, you're a stockbroker."

"What difference does it make?"

"I just like straight-forward talk, that's all."

"So you like straight-forward talk. Okay, then. See if this is straight forward enough for you. I think you're very pretty."

Sarah smiled, but didn't speak.

"And you shouldn't have told me about your skinny dipping. Now I can't get it out of my mind."

"Well, who knows? Maybe we'll come across another lake on the way down."

"As intriguing as that sounds, you're not in any condition for a swim, with or without a bathing suit."

Sarah laughed. "I know. I know. Anyway, I liked your nice compliment. So, Mr. Straight-Forward Investment Banker, I think we're going to get along just fine."

"I hate to tell you this, but you're not in a position to be picky about who might have happened along to help you."

"That's funny. I was thinking about that earlier. You're right of course."

She turned to look at him. "But I'm glad it's you."

Joel grinned. "Me, too."

Her thoughts returned momentarily to her disappointing relationship with Ryan.

Then for the first time, Sarah glanced down at his left hand. No ring. She smiled.

CHAPTER FIVE

When they set out again, she tightened her grasp around the back of his neck. After another hour on the trail, they stopped to rest again, sitting side by side on the trunk of a fallen tree.

Joel glanced at his watch. "I'd say we have another four hours to go. It'll be close, but I think we'll make it before dark."

She turned and gazed into his eyes. "Joel, will you kiss me?"

"Boy, you really aren't shy, are you?"

She didn't answer, but brushed her hair away from her face.

Joel turned toward her, put his hands on her shoulders, and kissed her long and passionately.

When they came up for air, Sarah sighed. "I asked you to kiss me, not make out with me."

"I didn't notice you resisting."

She put her hands on his chest and initiated another prolonged kissing session. When finally they resumed their descent, Sarah's mind was racing.

I know I just met this guy, but it's like I've known him for years. This could be the beginning of something special. I might look back on this as the day that changed my life.

Their next rest stop came after only thirty more minutes and before Joel could get his backpack off, Sarah snuggled into his body and kissed him long and hard.

Then she pulled away, looked at him and said, "Okay, we've determined that we're both straight-forward, right? So, Joel, have you ever been married?"

"Yes. I'm married now."

"What? But... so why...but you're not wearing a ring."

"I know. I'm not trying to fool people. I've just never worn rings. Never liked them."

"So why did you kiss me? Especially like that."

"Well, because you asked me to. It's not every day a beautiful woman asks me to kiss her."

"So let me guess. Your wife doesn't understand you and she treats you terribly, right?"

She wanted him to say "yes," and she would believe him because she so wanted it to be true. Or maybe they were separated. At the same time, she could just hear her friends telling her: *Sleep with whoever you want, but never, never, never get involved with a married man.*

"No, I wouldn't say that at all," Joel said. "Sorry, I wasn't trying to lead you on. And we were just kissing."

"*Just* kissing? I don't think I've ever been kissed like that before."

"Well, you deserve to be kissed like that—and often. It was special for me, too."

They hobbled down the trail in silence before stopping for another break by a gurgling stream.

Before they sat down, she said, "Okay, Mr. Straight-forward, *Married* Investment Banker, I still want you to kiss me some more."

He looked into her eyes. "Are you sure?"

She didn't answer and he put his arms around her and initiated a long, probing kiss. As they held each other tight, she could feel his arousal.

How can he kiss me like this and not want to be with me? "Joel, don't you feel we have a special connection? It's not just the kissing. It's the way we talk to each other. I feel like I've known you for years. I find myself telling you things I don't even tell my closest friends."

"I do, yes, but..."

"Are you sure you're married to the right woman? She must be this ugly witch who tricked you into marrying her, right?"

Joel laughed. "Well, you can decide for yourself. She should be waiting for us at the trailhead. We only have one car on this vacation and she agreed to pick me up. I'm sure she's wondering why I'm so late. Hopefully, she's not too worried."

Sarah stared at him. "Really, I'm going to have to meet your wife?"

"Yep. Don't worry, though, I doubt she'll cast any spells on you. She's not the jealous type. Although, when she gets a look at you...Well, you never know. We'll see."

When they were only a few minutes from the trailhead, Sarah asked if she could take a "selfie" of the two of them. "I, at least, want to remember this day and remember you."

"Of course, let's do it."

She took out her smart phone and he put his arm around her. They both smiled. After the photo, he kissed her on the cheek.

CHAPTER SIX

When they reached the parking lot, Sarah immediately saw a dark-haired woman running toward them.

"Joel, what happened? Are you alright?"

"I'm fine, but she's got a badly sprained ankle and it was a slow walk back."

"Hi, I'm Rachel. I'm glad Joel was there to help you."

Damn. Did she have to be so nice? "Me, too, I was a long ways up, and I'm not sure how I would have made it. Joel was a lifesaver."

"Do you want us to take you to the ER?"

"No, I don't want to go to the ER."

"Nobody *wants* to go to the ER, but maybe you should."

Sarah laughed. "No, I can drive myself home. I'll ice it and rest it and if it's not better in the morning, I'll have it looked at."

"Rach, I'll get Sarah to her car and I'll be right there."

When they were alone at her car, Sarah said, "You didn't tell me she was so gorgeous—and so nice."

"What can I say? Sarah, you're a very special woman and I know you're going to find someone. Someone other than your Ryan. Don't settle for less than you deserve."

He extended his hand and they shook. "Goodbye, Sarah Jenkins."

"Good bye, Joel Rosen. Thank you for getting me down. I am grateful for that—and your sweet kisses."

EPILOGUE

As Sarah drove home alone through the darkness, the throbbing in her ankle intensified. There was no flirtatious banter or passionate kisses to distract her.

Her thoughts again returned to her conversations with Joel about her relationship with Ryan.

Just a few hours ago, I thought this might be a day that would change the course of my life.

Maybe it was.

The End

THE
SERGEANT

CHAPTER ONE

JULY, 1969

Sergeant Sam Potter didn't fit in with his fellow black Marines. He talked slowly and deliberately. No jive talking. No black power fist salutes that were so prevalent on military outposts all across South Vietnam. He never participated in the racially divided groupings at mealtime. He sat where he wanted, often alone.

If it wasn't for his size—six-foot-six and two hundred and forty pounds—he might have been picked on mercilessly for not conforming. No one messed with Sgt. Potter, but it wasn't out of fear. He was respected. Compared to most of us in our unit, he was better educated and clearly an intellectual. He was a leader.

But on this day, it was obvious Sam was hurting. And that's where I come in. I was his best friend, and he was mine. Yeah, me, a white guy, Corporal Patrick O'Leary. He outranked me, but we treated each other as equals.

We often had long talks about politics, philosophy, the war and when it might end; and our shared love of Eddie Kendricks, Otis Williams, Paul Williams, Melvin Franklin and David Ruffin—The Temptations. And women. Well, me talking about women, he about his wife back home.

He had a photo of Arlene carefully preserved in a plastic sandwich bag. It was a side shot of her in a swim suit, sitting at the beach, showing off her long legs. I swear I saw him pull it out at least once or twice every day.

Beaming with pride, he would often show it to me. "Would you look at her?" he would say.

"Yeah, Sam, she's beautiful," I would answer as if I hadn't seen it dozens of times before.

Despite having to endure being thousands of miles from home, cold showers, tasteless rations, hot, steamy weather, and—oh, yeah, people trying to kill you—Sam was the most upbeat guy in the whole camp.

It was so out of character for him to seem the least bit down. But today there was something very, very wrong. There was no mistaking it, at least to me. So, when we were alone, I came right out and asked him.

"Sam, what's going on? Are you okay? Because you don't seem like yourself."

"I'm not sure I want to talk about it."

"Sam, it's me. You can tell me anything. You know that."

"It's Jody."

"Jody? Who in the hell is Jody?"

"You know, the Jody back home."

"Oh, that Jody."

We'd all heard the phrase a million times. Some Jody back home is fuckin' your girlfriend while you're over here fighting for your country. But, for Sam, it wasn't his girlfriend. It was his wife.

"How do you know?" I asked. "It's easy to get paranoid being so far away and having to listen to the way guys talk around here."

"I don't know, Pat. I can just tell. She doesn't write nearly as often, and when she does, I can read between the lines. Her tone is so different, not like before. She talks about getting together with friends and doing stuff. I can tell it's not just her girlfriends she's with. I think I'm losing her."

He choked up with emotion on his last words and then he did something I'd never seen him do. He cried.

"Listen, Sam, you've got to stay calm. Maybe you could write to her and sort all this out. I'm sure she loves you. She's probably just lonely and going out and having fun. That doesn't mean she's unfaithful."

"I wish I believed that. There's a Jody. I just know it."

"Okay, I won't argue with you, but, hey, you've got to stay cool. Tomorrow, we're heading out on a search-and-destroy mission and they say it could be a tough one—not that they're not always dangerous. So, we've got to keep our wits about us. When we get back to camp in a few days, we'll figure something out. I'll help you."

"You're right, I guess. There's nothing I can do about it from here anyway. If only I could get home, I think things would be all right. I'll be okay for tomorrow. Don't worry. Thanks for your support, man. I do appreciate it. You know that."

"I know."

CHAPTER TWO

We'd been sloshing through muddy jungle terrain for two days and still no sign of the enemy that "intelligence" said was in the area. Sam was leading our small patrol, only fifteen of us. We were in the middle of monsoon season, so the downpours never seemed to stop and the humidity was oppressive.

When someone complained, Sam would offer his usual optimism. "Hey, it's those buckets of rain that make this country so lush and scenic."

One guy yelled out, "Damn it, Sarge. Do you always have to be so fucking positive? Can't you let us wallow in our misery at least once in a while?"

Sam laughed, but didn't relent. "We need to be positive and stay focused if we're going to get through another day alive."

It was a typical Sam response, but this time he was faking it. He was still in pain, but only I could tell. I wasn't sure he even wanted to get through the day alive.

When we stopped in a clearing, the rain had turned into a light drizzle, but we were still huddled up in our ponchos, hoods up. We sat with our M-16s cradled in our laps while we quickly consumed cans of meat stew and beans. One of the guys who'd been standing guard interrupted our mealtime, violently waving his arms and silently pointing.

We jumped to our feet, rifles at the ready and peered into the brush. We heard movement. We knew it was most likely a small band of Viet Cong. Sam put his finger to his lips and motioned for us to stay low to the ground.

Within minutes, we could see figures sliding through the thick growth only a few yards away. Sam held up his hand and whispered, "Don't fire until I give the signal."

Then he used hand gestures to order four men in our squad to circle around to flank the V.C.

The firefight lasted about two hours. Miraculously, we didn't suffer any losses or injuries. We had launched about fifteen hand grenades onto their position. They apparently didn't have any. When Sam broke out of the clearing to assess the situation, he discovered ten Viet Cong bodies. The rest apparently had fled.

One of our squad members called out, "Sarge, I've got bad news. Perez is missing. I've combed the area and I can't find him anywhere."

"Joe's missing? Are you sure he wasn't shot?"

"I'm sure, Sarge. I think he may have been captured."

Sam looked to the sky for a few seconds, then said. "We're going after him. No one has to come. I want volunteers."

No one hesitated. We were all going. Each of us had probably suffered the nightmare of what it would be like to become a POW. We'd all heard the stories. We had to get Joe back. Our best chance to save him was to move quickly before he ended up in Hanoi.

On we trudged. The rain resumed its relentless downpour. After an hour, we could see there was a village ahead. It looked like a tiny one, only about twenty stilt huts with thatched roofs.

While we were stopped and Sam was planning our next move, a woman approached our position. One in our group was ready to shoot, but Sam held up his hand. "Keep a close eye on her movements, but let's see what she wants."

She was shaking, but through her broken English and gestures, we figured out she was tipping us off that Joe was being held by three Viet Cong in her village. She said they were waiting for North Vietnamese Army regulars to take custody and march him north. She stayed with us and, when we got to the edge of the ville, she pointed out the hut where Joe was being guarded.

The mini-battle was over in a flash. We rushed the hut, shot and killed the Viet Cong and freed Joe. Sam didn't hesitate. He fired the first shots. When the shooting stopped, one of our squad had grabbed a man, about sixty years old, and was holding him by the shirt collar.

"One of the villagers told me this guy is suspected of being a V.C. sympathizer. He may have been part of the bunch that attacked us earlier."

"Let him go," Sam said. "If we're not sure, we have to let him go. We got what we came for. Let's get outta here."

Most in our group were surprised, but not me. I knew Sam. He could kill without hesitation when he had to, but, if it wasn't absolutely necessary, he couldn't and wouldn't.

As I watched Sam that day it struck me how he could boldly overcome fear in the face of the enemy and possibly losing his life, but he was helpless to overcome the fear of losing his love. Maybe, unlike the rest of us, he had figured out at a very young age what was truly important in life.

I slapped him on the back. "Let's get back to camp, Sam. I've been thinking and I may have a solution to your problem."

His blank stare told me he was confused.

"You know—Jody."

"Oh, yeah. Jody. Really?"

"We'll talk when we get back."

As our tired group stumbled into camp, Sam was leading the singing of the "hook" to the Vietnam servicemen's anthem: "We've gotta get out of this place, if it's the last thing we ever do. We gotta get out of this place. Girl, there's a better life for me and you."

Of course, the song had nothing to do with the war, but we didn't care. We all wanted to go home, but for Sam it was becoming a necessity.

CHAPTER THREE

About halfway through my tour, I made the mistake of letting someone know I could type, so when we weren't on patrol, I was assigned to work in the company headquarters, a small hut with four desks, a file cabinet and a field phone. That gave me inside knowledge about the primitive communications systems employed in a war zone. It would be the key to getting Sam home.

My plan was simple. It just took guts and stupidity. I guess I had just enough of both. When I told Sam the plan, though, he said no way.

"If every guy who thought his girl was being screwed by some Jody got to go home, there'd be nobody left over here."

"But we're not talking about every guy. This is you and Arlene."

"I don't think I can do it, Pat. It's too risky."

"But that's just it. There's no risk and you don't have to do anything. I'll do it."

"You'd do this for me? I don't know. Go over the details again."

I'd seen the system work before, but legitimately. A first lieutenant's father had been near death and a military message—like a telegram—from the States was transmitted to Division Headquarters in Okinawa. It authorized orders to be cut to send him home.

From there, everything was transmitted down the line by radio-relay phones, from Okinawa to Battalion Headquarters and then into our little office. Our phone was a small, battery-operated device. It looked archaic. I swear it must have been left over from Iwo Jima.

Since, like Sam, the lieutenant had only a few months left on his Vietnam tour, he would not be sent back to the war after his leave, but would be re-assigned to stateside duty. The orders were issued the next day and the man was on his way home.

"It's not like it happens all the time, so no one's going to have any reason to doubt that it's legit. The simple truth, Sam, is that all of these messages are transmitted by phone, just like the one in our office. All I have to do is make the call right here after everyone's left for the day."

"Won't they know it's coming from here?"

"No. That's the whole point. The voices sound identical, no matter where they're coming from. The calls can't be traced."

"Really?"

"I'll say I'm in Admin at Division Headquarters. There's no reason anyone would question it. We just need a dramatic event. I'm thinking we say Arlene has been in a car crash and in critical condition. You've got a little less than a year left on your enlistment, so you'll have to be assigned to a permanent Marine

Corps base. We'll shoot for Camp Pendleton. That's fairly close to home, right?"

"Yeah, real close, but we could move to Oceanside, assuming we stay together."

"You'll stay together. I'm sure of it. I've heard you talk enough about Arlene to know you two were meant for each other. You'll work things out, Sam. I know you will."

"Thanks, man. I hope you're right. Okay, I'll do it. Are you sure you're—"

"I'm sure. Even if something goes wrong, no one will ever know who made the call, so you can't be blamed. There's really nothing to lose. You've done more than your part over here. Now it's time to go and take care of business at home."

Sam asked me if we should feel guilty about gaming the system. I told him to let me worry about that. I did feel guilty. For about thirty seconds.

CHAPTER FOUR

My call was answered quickly.

"Good afternoon, Battalion Headquarters, this is Lance Corporal Bailey."

Confidence was the main ingredient. I couldn't allow my voice to crack with nervousness. "Lance Corporal, this is Lieutenant Andersen in Admin at Third Marine Division."

"Yes, sir. What can I do for you?"

"I'm calling about one of the men in your outfit, a Sergeant Potter."

I could hear him shuffling papers. "Yes, sir, Sergeant Samuel Potter. He's in Alpha Company."

"We need you to cut orders for him to return to the States, ASAP. His wife has been in a car crash and she's in critical condition in a Los Angeles hospital. His orders should grant him two weeks leave, then assign him to Marine Corps Base Camp Pendleton."

"Yes, sir. I'll get these typed up, signed and messengered down right away. Then I'll call down to the company and have Sergeant Potter notified."

"Thanks, Bailey. Good job."

"Sir, does it make any difference if he goes on military or civilian aircraft?"

"No, just get him on the next flight out of Da Nang."

"Yes, sir. I'm on it. Anything else, sir?"

"No, that will be all and thanks again for your assistance, Lance Corporal."

"Yes, sir. You're welcome, sir."

Within twenty-four hours Sam was on a "Freedom Bird," heading home and that was that. I didn't hear from him, which wasn't a surprise. What was he going to do: write to thank me for cheating the system?

I missed our stimulating conversations and my last few months in Vietnam seemed to go slower. I was curious as to what happened to him and Arlene, but mostly I just missed our friendship.

I suppose it was based on a unique time in our lives. Being in our early twenties and in a war made our shared interests stand out. It was a time when you desperately wanted to find things you had in common, with no concerns about how different your backgrounds might be.

Given the racial divide of the times, I wondered if it would have been possible for us to be friends had we met back home. Would we have even met?

A few months later, when I had only eight days left on my tour, our base camp was attacked with a barrage of mortars. Nine guys were killed and another fifty-three, including me, were wounded.

My injuries were minor, only some shrapnel wounds in my arms and legs. A few inches either way and the flying metal would have blasted into my face and I would have been one of the KIAs. Those are the things that haunt you when it's all over.

When I first got home, I didn't think much about Sam. I had other things on my mind. I was glad to be a *former* Marine, with no worries about the draft lottery facing most of my friends. I was ready to put it all behind me. I was twenty-one and alive. I'd made it and it was time to start my life.

Some of my friends were impressed that I was awarded a Purple Heart, but they didn't understand you didn't have to do anything heroic to get one. You just had to get hurt. The real heroes were the guys who didn't come back. I was glad Sam wasn't one of those. Maybe I was a hero to Sam. I could always hold on to that, but I figured I'd never know.

As years went by, I began to feel a sense of pride that I'd done my part. I even framed my Purple Heart and other Vietnam service medals. And I began to think more and more about Sam and others I had served with.

When the Internet came along, I realized there was a chance I could locate him. There were dozens of sites designed for vets to hook up with their old units, but they never worked for me, although every few years I would make another attempt.

Finally, I gave up and was resigned to the fact that I would never see Sam again and never know how his life turned out.

EPILOGUE

It had been nearly fifty years since my time in Vietnam. I still thought about Sam and wondered about him and Arlene and if he had achieved his dreams of finishing his last two years at UCLA and getting into law school.

Then one day, a trip to the mailbox brought tears to my eyes. It's rare these days to get old-fashioned mail of any kind. So it was especially shocking to see a hand-addressed envelope with my name written as "Corporal Patrick O'Leary." I didn't recognize the return address, but it was from Ventura, California. My pulse raced. Could it be?

Dear Pat,

I am so glad I finally found you and I hope you're in good health, at least for an old guy. Can you believe we're now in our seventies?

I tried to find you many times on Internet sites, but I had no success. And when I saw your name on the Vietnam Wall, I thought you must have been killed in the attack on our compound that occurred after I left.

Then, I was able to get in touch with some of the other guys in our unit. You remember Perez? He's the guy we rescued from the Viet Cong that day. Anyway, he told me that it must have been another Patrick O'Leary on the wall, because he was sure you had survived the attack and were medevaced home.

I would have called, but I could only find your address. These days, you probably only have a cell phone. Maybe it's just as well, as I can better express my thoughts in writing. Hopefully, this won't seem too mushy for a couple of ex-Marines.

I have never forgotten you or what you did for me. It changed my life. It's a long story, but Arlene and I were able to stay together. I'll spare you the details for now, but it was a rough go for a while. Today, we have two sons, a daughter and six grandkids.

I would love to see you and hear about your life. I'm winding down my law practice, so I have plenty of time. I'd love to have you stay with us. I've got plenty of Temptations songs on my iPod. Let me know, old friend.

Sincerely,
Sam Potter

At the bottom of the letter, was a phone number. Within minutes, I was on the phone chatting with Sam as if we talked every week. Within an hour, I bought an airline ticket to California.

Amazingly, our wartime friendship had transcended time, distance and race.

The End

THE
GUNFIGHT

CHAPTER ONE

It was three in the afternoon. Main Street was nearly deserted. The only sound was heavy boots crunching on dirt and gravel. The four men weren't in any hurry. Their pace was methodical.

Each carried six-shooters tucked in their belts. Two cradled shotguns. There'd be no backing down. Today this would be settled once and for all.

The bystanders who had gathered along the wood sidewalks were curious, but silent as the group passed the telegraph office, the bank, then the hotel and saloon. The October sun was bright, so the long black coats caused the determined gun toters to sweat. Silver badges were pinned on two of the men's outerwear.

A hundred yards away at the opposite end of the street, another foursome appeared, walking at the same steady pace toward the others. Three wore cowboy hats and were armed with pistols and shotguns. One carried his weapon in a traditional gun belt and holster with bullets filling the loops all around the belt.

The fourth was staggering and had a bandage around his head. He carried a Winchester rifle.

"Here they come," someone yelled. A five-year-old boy darted into the street after the lawmen had passed his position. A young mother dashed out and scooped him up. "Johnny, what are you doing? Get back here."

As the two factions drew closer, the bandaged cowboy yelled at one of the lawmen. "You coward! You pistol-whipped me from behind this morning. Now you think you're a big man because you've got your brothers with you. Well, you're not going to get away with your tough-guy routine anymore. This is the day you die."

The verbal assault was returned in kind. "You're drunk, as usual, and you've been bragging all morning how you're gonna kill me. Now you're gonna get your chance. You damn cowboys are all alike. You think you're above the law."

"We're cattlemen. We're legitimate businessmen. We moved out here so we wouldn't have government freeloaders like you telling us what to do. We're the ones who tamed this territory. It's *you* and your kind who think you're above the law just because you're wearing badges. You've abused your authority far too long. Today it ends."

The tallest of the lawmen shouted, "Listen carefully. We represent the citizens of this town. We intend to disarm you. So throw up your hands and put down your weapons. Now!"

"We will not," shouted one of the cowboys.

Suddenly, all talk ceased as each side stared at the other. They were now only about twenty feet apart. More bystanders had gathered along both sides of the dusty street.

Then someone's hand moved toward a pistol crammed into the waistband of his pants, and the shooting started. The gunshots were deafening. Some of the bystanders held their hands to their ears.

One of the cowboys clutched his stomach and fell to the ground. One of the lawmen grabbed his leg and crumpled to the dirt. Within seconds, it was over and all four cowboys were down and motionless.

Then one of the lawmen cautiously walked over to one of the fallen men. He looked down momentarily, extended his arm and opened his hand. The man on the ground smiled, grabbed his hand and pulled himself up.

Loud applause was heard all around as the eight men patted one another on the back.

A woman and her two children rushed over to the actors. "Can we get a photo?"

"Of course. Just give us a minute."

When the group was assembled with the children in front, the re-enactment team, staying in character, maintained stern looks.

The mother pulled out her smart phone. "Okay, smile, everyone."

"We are smiling," one of the actors said with a frown.

After several rounds of photos, Josh Haller, the man who had portrayed the drunk, removed his gun belt. "Let's get this stuff put away. Jessie's saving a table for us up at the bar. I don't know about you guys, but I'm thirsty. It's Friday. Come on, what d' ya say?"

Kevin McGee was the first to speak up. "So what if it's Friday; we still have to work tomorrow. But sure, I'm up for it. Let's go, guys."

The rest of the troupe readily agreed.

CHAPTER TWO

How could one stupid song cause a man so much heartache? That's what Kevin was wondering as he strolled toward the bar at the other end of town. Yes, there it was again, running through his head over and over. He never liked it when it came out in the 80s and he absolutely hated it now, but it was always there, haunting him.

Jessie's got himself a girl and I want to make her mine. I wish that I had Jessie's girl. I wish that I had Jessie's girl.

No, his friend's name wasn't Jessie. It was Josh. They weren't that close really, but they did work together every day. And it wasn't Josh's girl that Kevin wished he had; she was his *wife*. The terrible irony was that *her* name was Jessie. And just like the song lyrics said, she was just loving Josh with that gorgeous body of hers. He just knew it.

So, there it was. He had to listen to the song in his head every time he was about to see her. As usual, he thought about staying away from her, but he always ended up changing his mind. The agony of the song and the situation were worth it. He just loved being around her, even if he couldn't have her.

As he got closer, he pictured how beautiful she was and what she might be wearing. Probably tight black jeans and a cowgirl blouse, maybe even a cowboy hat, with her light brown, shoulder-length hair flowing out from underneath.

It's too bad we can't figure out some way to have a woman in our little skit. She would so look the part of the sexy, but tough cowgirl.

But he mostly thought about her infectious smile and gregarious laugh. She was always the life of the party—very talkative, but never in a frivolous way. When she asked a question, she seemed genuinely interested in the answer.

I know she likes me. She's always so nice to me. Why couldn't I have met her first? I know we'd be good together. And when I see her with Josh... They just don't seem right for each other. For one thing, she's taller than him, for crying out loud. She'd look more natural standing next to me.

When he entered the building, he saw the group at the rear of the room. Ten couples were chatting away and pitchers of beer dotted the long table. When Jessie spotted Kevin, she was the first to greet him. "Hey, Kev, glad you made it." She gave him a big hug. "I was afraid you weren't coming."

"Why wouldn't I come, Jess? You know I can't resist our after-work parties."

Josh was already a couple of mugs of beer into the celebration. "Hey, anyone up for the game room? I challenge anyone here to a foosball match. Come on, Kev. How about it?"

"No. Maybe later. I'd hate for you to start your night on a losing streak."

"Big talk for someone who's afraid to play. That's okay. How about you, Jess?"

"No thanks, Hon."

"That's okay. You stay here and keep this chicken company."

Most of the gang followed Josh, with just one couple remaining at the far end of the table.

"Geez, Kev, I guess it's just you and me. That's fine. I've been meaning to ask you about your latest career plans."

"Career? What career?"

"You know, acting. What's your dream? Hollywood? Broadway?"

"Honestly, I don't really consider myself an actor. Sure, I did drama in high school, and I do try to give each performance my best shot, but for me this is just a job, not a career path."

"But you're really talented."

"I honestly don't think I'm that good and I'm not just being modest. Even if that were true, I'm not really sure what I want to do. Right now, it's just a fun gig in a fun place. I love being in the great outdoors all year-'round, away from a big city. Even though it's just a re-creation to attract tourists, I still like the feeling of being in a small town in the Old West."

"Well, as long as you don't go shootin' up the town like you boys do in your little street skit."

"Don't worry about that. Actually, I do like shooting for real, though. With real guns."

"I thought you guys did use real guns."

"That's true, but you know what I mean. I mean with real bullets, not blanks. I was thinking of going hunting this weekend, but I'm not sure if I'll get the chance. So, what about *your* career? I'm guessing you don't want to be a soda fountain waitress forever."

"It's not a bad job, actually. The tips are good and the customers are always so friendly."

"Yeah, well, they might not be as friendly if the girl behind the counter wasn't so pretty."

She blushed. "Seriously, they're always in a good mood and it's so nice to see families having fun together and couples holding hands. Vacations seem to put people in a positive frame of mind."

"But don't you think it will get old eventually?"

"Probably, but for now, I just like being out here, like you said. As long as we can make enough to get by, the lifestyle is great. Josh and I are young, still in our twenties for a few more years. Same as you, right?"

"Yeah, but I'm turning twenty-seven next month, well on my way to that dreaded thirty."

"I *thought* you had a birthday coming up. We'll have to have a party."

"No need, really, but thanks, Jess. So you guys think you'll stick around here for a while?"

"I'm not sure. I don't know. Josh isn't a very good communicator, so I never know for sure what he wants or what our future might look like. Sometimes, I wonder—" Her eyes got misty.

"Wonder what, Jess?"

"Nothing. We've only been married for three months. In a way, we're still getting to know each other and what we want. We got married awfully fast—a whirlwind romance. Anyway, I hope you'll stick around here at least as long as we're here. It wouldn't be the same without you. You're a special friend." She paused. "To both me and Josh. I know he thinks a lot of you."

Kevin's face lit up. "Thanks, Jess. You, too."

As the foosball players rejoined the table, Jessie raised her voice. "Everyone's invited over to our place tonight for pizza."

She turned to Kevin. "You'll come, won't you?"

"Well, I don't know. I really should—"

"Come on Kevin, you have to come. Please."

Josh, overhearing the conversation, turned to Kevin. "Yeah, Kevin, come. It'll be fun. If Jessie says you need to be there, then you need to be there."

Josh turned to say good-bye to the others in the group without waiting for an answer. Kevin was always surprised at Josh's lack of jealousy. No matter how much time he spent talking to Jessie, her husband never seemed to notice.

Kevin turned to Jess. "Okay, I'll be there."

CHAPTER THREE

Main Street was nearly deserted. The only sound was heavy boots crunching on dirt and gravel. The four men weren't in any hurry. Their pace was methodical. Each carried six-shooters tucked in their belts. Two cradled shotguns. There'd be no backing down. Today this would be settled once and for all.

Since this was a morning performance, it was cooler and the long coats weren't such a burden.

When Josh clutched his stomach and fell to the ground in the finale, Kevin followed the script and sauntered over, stood over his victim and reached out to lift him up.

After a few quick bows, acknowledging the applause, Kevin turned to Josh. "Hey, when we get done with the afternoon show, do you want to go shooting out in the desert?"

"Sure, why not? Is it okay if Jess comes? She's always saying she wants to see if us cowpokes can really hit anything."

"Yeah, of course. Bring her along."

Kevin turned to the others. "Anyone else up for some desert shooting practice? There's a batch of dead saguaros that'll make good targets."

Jack Lewis, who portrayed one of the cowboys, walked closer to Kevin. "I'd love to come, but I don't own a gun. In fact, I've never shot before, except in our little play here."

"Not a problem," Kevin said. "We'll take one of these. In fact, you can use the one I use in the show. It's an authentic Colt .45. I've got live ammo for it."

"Really?" Jack said. "I didn't know these were even real weapons."

"You bet they're real. That's why we need to check them before every show to make sure they have blanks. Anyway, you should join us. It'll be fun. And I'd be glad to offer you a lesson—after some quick safety tips."

A ten-year-old girl interrupted the conversation by tugging on Kevin's overcoat. "Can we take our picture with you?"

"Sure. Come on, guys. We're not done yet. Let's do the photos."

CHAPTER FOUR

Bam, bam, bam. Kevin fired off three shots in quick succession. All three were direct hits on the prickly target about a hundred yards from where the shooters were positioned.

"So you really *can* shoot," Jessie said. "Josh said you were good, but I had to see for myself."

"Been doing it since I was a kid. My dad got me into hunting when I was about twelve. Jack, you ready for a go?"

"I'm ready, but after watching you load those cartridges—well, I'm curious about something. How can you tell a real bullet from a blank?"

"Let me take that one," Josh said. "Jack, let's step over here. We'll let Jess go next and I'll offer you a quick tutorial. First of all, most people get confused about the terms. A bullet is not the same as a cartridge. The bullet is actually *inside* the cartridge. For the show, we use the same cartridges, but with no bullets inside."

"So how does it make so much noise?"

"Because we use real gunpowder and the explosion is real. In fact, we use a little extra to get that super

117

loud crack that makes the audience jump. But take a look. On the live ammo, you can see the projectile sticking out, but on the blanks, it's level."

"So, with no bullet, there's absolutely no danger?"

"Not exactly. One time, some dumb-shit movie actor blew his brains out with a blank."

"What?"

"Yeah, the explosion still has tremendous force. This idiot was joking around and put the gun to his head and fired. Pieces of his skull went into his brain and he died."

Jack shook his head.

Bam, bam, bam, bam, bam. Jessie took her turn. Five straight hits. "See, I can shoot pretty darn good myself, Mr. Lawman."

Kevin didn't see the bullets rip into the cactus. His eyes were glued on Jessie, wishing he could take her in his arms and kiss her passionately. Hearing her voice, he quickly turned to see the results.

"You're a great shot. I'm not surprised, Jess."

When everyone had their fill of shooting, Josh hauled the cooler from the Explorer. "Hey, Kevin, is it okay to break out the beer now?"

"Go head. But first, let me get these guns and ammo out of the way. Accidents do happen. Booze and guns don't mix, ya know. Safety first, Josh."

"I know. I know. That's what I like about you, Kev. You're always organized and making sure we do things right."

"Well, someone's got to do it."

"Here, let me help," Jessie said.

"Great. Thanks."

"If you want, Josh and me can return this stuff to the office. It's right on our way and he's got a key."

"No, that's okay. I need to go into the office anyway. I need to check next week's schedule. Thanks, though."

With the tailgate down, the two stashed the weapons in the back.

"Wait, I forgot to switch out the ammo in my Peacemaker."

Jessie watched as he removed the live ammunition from the show gun, making sure the chamber was empty as well. He loved Jess standing so close to him. He reached into the box of blanks and grabbed a handful. He could smell her wonderful scent and wished he could grab her and kiss her right then and there.

He jiggled a set of cartridges in each hand, one live and one with blanks. He paused and looked back and forth at each handful. Jessie looked from his hands to his face. She noticed moisture forming on his forehead. She stared, wide-eyed at Kevin. He didn't notice her gaze.

She turned away and shouted, "Hey, Josh, open one for me. Did anyone bring something to eat?"

CHAPTER FIVE

It was cloudy with the threat of rain. Main Street was nearly deserted. The only sound was heavy boots crunching on dirt and gravel. The actors seemed a bit lethargic today, but the audience couldn't tell.

They passed the telegraph office, the bank, then the hotel and saloon.

Josh adjusted the bandage on his forehead, then yelled, "You coward. You pistol-whipped me from behind this morning. Now you think you're a big man because you've got your brothers with you. Well, you're not going to get away with your tough-guy routine anymore. This is the day you die."

Kevin's retort came on cue. "We intend to disarm you. So throw up your hands and put down your weapons. Now!"

"We will not," Josh shouted.

Then Jack's hand moved toward a pistol crammed into the waistband of his pants and the shooting started. Kevin lifted his Colt .45 Peacemaker and fired off his usual five or six shots toward Josh. He wondered why the bangs weren't as loud as they usually were.

Josh clutched his stomach and fell to the ground. One of the lawmen actors grabbed his leg and also fell. Within seconds, it was over and all four cowboys were down and not moving.

Kevin gave the audience time to absorb the action and begin their applause, then strolled over to Josh and extended his arm to help him up. Josh didn't move and that's when Kevin saw the blood dripping from the chest area of his shirt.

Kevin's thoughts were firing through his brain at the speed of a bullet. *Oh, my God, he's shot. I've shot him. How did—I didn't mean to do it. Did I?*

He remembered back to the previous afternoon when he was putting the guns away after the desert outing. While the others had been drinking and not looking, he'd filled his gun with real bullets. But back at the office, he changed his mind. He had carefully unloaded the live bullets and hurriedly grabbed the empty cartridges from a nearby box, shoved them into the pistol, then almost ran out the door.

I know I put the blanks back in the gun. I'm sure I did. What if he's dead? Did I do it on purpose? Maybe I did load the real bullets and my mind is playing tricks on me. What have I done? God, help me.

Jack was the first to scramble to Josh's side. "Someone call 911," he yelled. "Josh has been shot—for real. Call 911."

Gasps could be heard from the audience. Then a woman raced toward Josh. "I'm a doctor, move aside and let me have a look."

The other actors gathered around Josh, but widened their circle to allow room for the doctor. Within minutes, a siren wailed in the distance, but it was too late.

"I'm afraid he's gone," the doctor pronounced.

Kevin was shaking. *I can't believe this is happening. I swear I put the blanks in. I don't know. I'm so confused. This can't be happening. I'm feeling dizzy. Either way, I've killed him and it's my fault. It was an accident. I know it was. But will people believe me? What will Jess think? Will she think I killed him on purpose? Oh, my God, someone's got to tell Jess. Who will tell Jess?*

He fell to his knees in anguish, clutched his gun, stared at the six-shooter in disbelief and yelled. "My God, I didn't know there was live ammo in my gun. He was my friend. How can he be dead?"

He covered his face with both hands and sobbed, tears streaming down his cheeks. His fellow actors gathered around him and helped him up. "It's okay, Kevin. We know you didn't mean to. It was a tragic accident. Come with us. We'll stay with you until the sheriff gets here."

* * *

Jess looked up when the deputy sheriff entered the ice cream parlor. She could tell from the look on his face that he wasn't there to order a chocolate malt.

She cried, but didn't become hysterical.

"I thought they always checked the weapons before every show. How did it happen?"

"We're not sure, ma'am. There will be an investigation, of course, but we don't really know much now—except that somehow there were live bullets in one of the guns and your husband was killed. I'm terribly sorry, ma'am. Is there someone I can call to be with you, or can I give you a ride somewhere?"

She didn't ask who fired the shots.

"Do I need to identify the body?"

"No, that won't be necessary. You're welcome to come to the mortuary when the coroner is finished, but several of his friends were there, so we know it was Josh. I am so sorry, Mrs. Haller."

"Where's the rest of the troupe? Was anyone arrested?"

"I assume they're all down at the station, giving statements. That's all I know."

CHAPTER SIX

THREE DAYS LATER

From the *News-Gazette*

Shooting Skit Gone Wrong
Leaves One Actor Dead

Josh Haller, 25, a local actor, was killed Tuesday during a gunfight re-enactment skit on Main Street. Sheriff Cal Jensen said the death is under investigation.

"The performance came off normally, as it does every day, but somehow, one of the guns had live bullets and Mr. Haller was hit with four shots," Jensen said. "A fifth bullet ended up in the side of the outer wall of the bank." He said no bystanders were injured.

The shots were fired by Haller's good friend and fellow actor, Kevin McGee, according to Jensen. He said the shooting appeared to be accidental, but that didn't preclude the possibility of charges being filed against McGee or the show's owners for negligence.

Haller, originally from Sioux Falls, S.D., had been with Gunslinger Productions, Inc. for the past three years, according to a company spokesperson.

The day after the shooting, the Town Council met in emergency session and voted unanimously to suspend all further gun skits until new safety inspection rules could be drawn up and implemented.

"This is a real tragedy, not only for Josh's family, but also for the whole community," Mayor Jim Redding said. "We realize these shows and the tourists they bring to town are an important part of our local economy, but the safety of the performers and the audiences must come first."

Redding said it was everyone's hope that the shows would resume in the not-too-distant future.

Mr. Haller is survived by his wife Jessica; his parents, John and Alice Haller of Sioux Falls and a sister Louise Keller of Branson, Missouri. Services have not yet been scheduled.

SIX MONTHS LATER

From the *News-Gazette*

No Charges Filed in Shootout; Death Ruled Accidental

After a six-month review, the County Attorney's office has decided not to file charges in the death of Josh Haller, who was killed during a shootout re-enactment on Main Street last October.

Haller and fellow actor Kevin McGee were facing off in one of the town's many simulated gunfights when

McGee fired five live rounds. Four struck Haller and he was pronounced dead at the scene.

Following a preliminary investigation, Sheriff Cal Jensen determined the shooting was an aggravated assault due to recklessness. But County Attorney Sam Green said, "This incident was tragic, but the evidence shows it was an accident and not a crime. No charges will be filed."

Green said the gun involved in the shooting had been used for target practice the day before and that live ammunition was inadvertently left in the weapon.

Green also said that all shows involving guns need to employ better safety measures and the town already has taken steps to ensure that will be the case in the future.

Immediately following the incident, all shooting skits were temporarily banned. The Town Council later passed an ordinance requiring permits and more stringent weapon checks before each show.

Jessica Haller, widow of the deceased actor, said she had no comment on the county attorney's announcement.

CHAPTER SEVEN

When he finished reading the story, Kevin was overcome with relief. He wept.

I've got my life back. My friends don't think I'm a killer, and now the authorities don't think I'm a killer either.

But within an hour, the old doubts and feelings of guilt returned with a vengeance. One person his acting hadn't totally convinced was himself.

I did think about doing it and it did happen. That can't be a coincidence. How can I still be so confused? Those few seconds when I decided what to do are such a blur.

At the moment of his greatest agony he knew who could help. Jessie. He had to talk to Jessie. He now had an overpowering compulsion to talk to her. He suddenly had to know whether the person whose opinion mattered the most thought he was a killer.

He had only talked to her briefly at the funeral. He had wanted to see her and spend time with her more than anything, but, in spite of his emotional state, he still had the presence of mind to know that any contact with her would only create gossip, or worse, cause the authorities to be suspicious. He had written her a long letter, but ripped it up.

Within a week after the shooting, he moved to Tucson and found temporary work, promising the sheriff he would come back at any time for more questioning if necessary.

It should be safe now. I've got to see her. I've got to know how she feels about everything and she needs to hear my version of what happened—not just read what others say in the newspaper. I owe her that.

Within an hour, he was in his car and on the highway. Four hours later, he was at her front door.

CHAPTER EIGHT

Holding the folded newspaper in one hand, he knocked on her door with the other. She answered within seconds and immediately put her arms around him and hugged hard.

"Kevin. I'm so glad to see you. I've missed you so much. I've been dying to talk to you, but I know why you didn't call. I understand. It was the right thing to do, but it was so hard. I've been so worried about you."

"Gosh, Jess, this is exactly the reception I was hoping for—even better really. I've missed you, too, and I think about you all the time, with everything that you're going through. And I didn't know how much you blamed me for what happened."

"But you saw the story in the paper, so—"

He held up the paper. "Of course I saw it. At first I was so happy. Then I realized I still didn't know how *you* felt."

"I never blamed you, not ever. It was an accident, pure and simple. I've had lots of support from family and friends. Josh's family has been especially attentive. I'm doing fine, but I really missed you. I mean it."

Josh. He had barely thought about Josh. Strangely, he almost didn't think of Jessie as Josh's widow. He only thought about her as the woman he loved and the woman he was forced to stay away from for far too long.

"Jess, I can't tell you how much this means to me. Your reaction is more than I could have hoped for."

"Hey, Kevin, I've got a question that I've been meaning to ask you. And don't laugh. Do you remember the song *Jessie's Girl* by Rick Springfield?"

"I do and I hate that song."

"I do, too, actually, but I could swear I heard you humming and singing parts of it a few times in the weeks before Josh was killed."

"It's always running through my head. You know how that goes."

"Yeah, I guess I do." She looked intently into his eyes.

"Okay, I admit it. I've had a crush on you for as long as I can remember."

"A crush?"

"Okay, it's more than a crush. I'll just say it. I'm totally, head over heels, hopelessly in love with you. Didn't you know that?"

"Of course I knew you were in love with me, and I so wanted you to be."

"Really?"

"You couldn't tell the feeling was mutual?"

"Well, I hoped, and I knew we got along so well, but..."

"Now let me tell you something. I knew I'd made a big mistake about a month after Josh and I got married. And you were always there. It was you I looked forward to seeing. It was you I fantasized about when we were apart."

She pressed her body into his and kissed his lips, then grabbed his hand and gently tugged, leading him into her bedroom.

* * *

Afterwards, she snuggled into his body and they dozed in and out of light, blissful sleep. Finally, she slid away and leaned on her elbow.

"Wow. Kev, I always knew it could be like this—that it *should* be like this. I could actually feel how much you love me with each kiss and every touch." She giggled. "And with each thrust. You're a fantastic lover, very passionate and so unselfish."

"Jess, I don't think it's me so much. We're just so good together. We were meant to be together. I wish I'd met you before Josh did."

"Me, too."

Kevin sat up and stared into her eyes. "Jess, I need to ask you something, though. We haven't really talked about Josh and—"

"Kevin, it's okay. We don't need to—"

"No, I need to get this off my chest. I need to ask you. What if I did something that was totally unforgiveable? Could you still forgive me?"

"Of course, I could, but—"

"No wait, just listen, please. I've never been sure what happened with the bullets and blanks and I was thinking—"

"Kevin, stop. Just stop a minute. There's nothing to forgive. You didn't do it."

"But, Jess—"

"Kevin, I'm telling you, you didn't do it. I did it."

"What? What are you talking about? That's ridiculous."

"I did it. I must have done it. Just listen to me. That afternoon when we were all shooting at the saguaros, when you were putting the guns away, remember?"

"Of course. How could I forget? It's those few seconds that I can't get out of my mind."

She gently touched his arm. "I was there next to you and I could see what you were thinking, even while Josh was explaining to Jack about how blanks work. But there's a long way between fleetingly thinking of doing something evil and actually doing it.

"I knew you couldn't go through with it. That's just not who you are. So later that night, when Josh was asleep, I took his key and I sneaked into the office. I was right. You *had* put the blanks back in your pistol. So, I switched them."

"Jess, what are you saying? You can't mean it. You're just trying to ease my guilt."

"No, I'm telling you the truth. I put the real bullets in your gun." Tears began to trickle down her cheeks and her voice shook.

"But like you, I changed my mind and switched them back—or at least I thought I did. I must not have. I don't know. I'm confused. I must have killed Josh. But for sure, you didn't do it. So, Kevin, now the question is…can you forgive *me*?"

He stared at her for several seconds and squirmed in the bed. After a long, uncomfortable silence, he finally spoke.

"No, Jess, I don't think I can. It doesn't make sense. In a twisted way, it made more sense that I would have killed him so you would turn to me. It would have been wrong, but it would have made more sense. But you—you could have just divorced him if you wanted to be with me."

"But, Kev, think about what just happened, not just the sex. We're connected in a special way. You know we are. I've never experienced anything like it and I don't think you have either."

She leaned in to kiss his lips, but he turned away.

"I'm not a murderer. That's not who I am. Thanks to you, I now know that for sure."

He took a deep breath and admired her beautiful body. "But, Jess, no matter how good we are together, this isn't going to work. We both had murder in our hearts. There's something wrong here. This is no way to start a relationship. Maybe we're not meant to be together after all."

He got dressed while Jess continued to plead with him. As he left the bedroom, Jess, wrapped a bed sheet around her naked body and followed him to the front door.

"Kevin, wait, please. Don't go. At least stay and talk this out. Don't leave me like this. We were meant to be together. You said so yourself. Please."

Kevin looked over his shoulder as he walked down the sidewalk toward the street. "Good bye, Jessie."

As he walked toward his car, there were no songs running through his head.

EPILOGUE

As he walked up the sidewalk to Jessie's door, he thought about how he was now lucky enough to have a date with the woman he had desired for so long.

Well, my plan didn't work out exactly as I had hoped. Josh is gone and Kevin should have been charged with his murder, but at least he's out of the picture now anyway.

Sure, I knew he had a crush on Jessie. Hell, who didn't? Half the men in this town wanted her. And everyone could see how she felt about him. They were constantly flirting. The only one stupid enough not to see it was Josh.

But I knew that neither Kevin or Jessie would have the guts to switch the cartridges, so I had to do it myself. How could they not know that I had a key to the office, too?

He knocked on the door, and she answered quickly, "Hi. You're early. Come on in and sit down, Jack. I'll be ready in just a few minutes."

The End

THE COIN
TOSS

CHAPTER ONE

Fred had never been in the Oval Office, but he wasn't all that impressed. It was exactly like the recreations in so many movies and TV shows he'd seen over the years. While waiting, he thought back to the time when he and President Connelly were both political novices, wading through mundane zoning and budget issues on the City Council.

The president bounded in through one of the side doors. "Fred Otterberg, how are you? It's been way too long."

"Mr. President."

"Call me Ken, please."

"But—"

"No, I insist. It's Ken. We go back way too far for it to be anything else. Besides I won't be president much longer, only a few more months."

"Okay. Ken it is. Good to see you."

"Now that you've seen the Oval Office, let's go into my real office. This place is just for show—and maybe a few meetings."

He led the way through the same door where he had entered. The small, wood-paneled, windowless room had a small desk, two visitors' chairs and two bookcases. One was filled with books, the other with photos and memorabilia.

"It's small, but just right for me. I've got my laptop and my music and a few personal items. It's a place where I can be by myself and just think."

"Very nice. It does seem like you. So, why did you invite me here anyway?"

"As you know, I'm at the end of my second term and I truly am planning to ride off into the sunset. I've given this a lot of thought. There'll be no paid speeches, no book tours, no convention appearances.

"This is really it. Suzie and I have talked it over and we really want to return to private life after thirty years in the public eye. So, I've had this overwhelming urge to see and thank some of the folks who were there at the beginning, and you, more than anyone else, were there at the *very* beginning."

"I guess that's true. I've been proud to support you all these years, even though we belong to different parties. I haven't agreed with all of your policies, but I do think you've been good for the country overall. You've restored honesty, character and integrity to the White House. That's what's made you such a popular president."

"Yeah, sometimes I can't really believe my own poll numbers, but you know as much as anyone how a politician's public image—good or bad—isn't always accurate. The voters feel like they know someone, but how can they really? Certainly not from news stories and thirty-second ads, but that's the way our system works and it's all we've got.

"Politics may be part skill, but it could be more a question of good timing and a whole lot of good luck, or at least the absence of *bad* luck. You can stub your toe and you'll never be president. One wrong vote or one stupid quote and you're done."

"You're right. That's one of the reasons I'm not sorry my time in politics was fairly short."

"But, Fred, it might have been different. You know that. This might have been you."

"I'm not so sure about that. Besides, you had the better political name—Ken Connelly. An alliteration, very catchy. Most presidents had short, simple, easy to pronounce names. Bush, Carter, Adams, Grant."

"What about Washington?"

"Longer, true, but not exactly a tongue-twister."

"Eisenhower. What about Eisenhower?"

"You got me there, but still, when you're the guy who won World War II…"

"Hey, you've obviously given this topic some thought—studying the length of names of presidents. I'm impressed."

"Well, as you know it's hard to get politics out of your system once you've been bitten by the bug. When I got out, I always joked that I was a recovering politician, but it really wasn't a joke. But the extent of politics in my life now is reading the paper and jawing with the guys I meet for coffee every morning at the corner diner.

"Sure, I enjoyed serving on the Council. We did have fun times, you and me, but I've never regretted my decision to get out. Mr.—Ken, you seem a bit nervous.

Are you sure there isn't something else? Another reason you invited me to the White House?"

"Fred, do you remember the coin toss?"

"Of course I remember the coin toss. How could I forget? It changed both of our lives."

CHAPTER TWO

TWENTY-FIVE YEARS EARLIER

As Ken sipped his coffee at the breakfast table, he tried to focus on the kids, but it was hard. It wasn't just the crucial budget vote on today's Council agenda. In fact, what was happening today at City Hall wasn't even on the agenda, yet it could change the way the rest of his life played out.

It had only been a week since the funeral services for the long-time, popular mayor; and the battle to see which council member would become acting mayor had already grown intense.

It was down to three of the seven council members. Fred, the longest-serving council member and Ken's closet ally on the Council, seemed like the obvious choice. Walt, the man who Ken and Fred thought was always on the wrong side of every important issue, was campaigning hard for the job. Ken was the third candidate.

Throwing his hat in this small ring wasn't a foregone conclusion. He and Suzie had all but decided that he would not run for re-election and he'd resume his career in advertising. Janie and Ron were growing up fast and, at forty, he had only so many years left to start putting away some serious money for college.

"Let's give this one last shot," he had told his wife. "If I don't win, that's okay. We've got each other. You and the kids are the most important thing in the world to me. I don't *have* to be in politics to have a good life."

Suzie wasn't so sure. Serving in public office had been his lifelong dream, but she readily agreed with his do-or-die plan. She wanted him to win, but down deep she wondered if they might have a better life if he lost. And they both knew the odds of his becoming mayor weren't that good.

The three contenders seemed hopelessly deadlocked in their quest for four votes. Each had only one committed supporter, plus their own vote. Getting two more votes seemed insurmountable with only one Council member in the undecided column.

So his meeting with Fred this morning could be crucial. He and Fred could talk frankly, even though they were both competing for the same prize. There must be a way they could work something out.

Suzie stood next to the breakfast table where Ken was chatting with Janie and Ron. "Are you sure you don't want some eggs? I'm scrambling some for the kids anyway."

"No, I'm fine, but thanks. Big day today. I need to stick with my regular fruit and cereal."

Turning to his seven-year-old, he asked, "So, Janie, what's happening for you at school today? Anything special?"

"No, not really, but Daddy, before you go to work, can I show you this magic trick I've been practicing?"

"I don't know. How about you show it to me tonight? I'll have much more time. I promise."

"But it will only take a minute. Please, Daddy. Please."

"Okay, but hurry."

When he finished breakfast, he mustered all of his concentration to focus on Janie's trick. When she had finished, he clapped enthusiastically, then leaned down and kissed her on the cheek before heading for his car.

CHAPTER THREE

Ken burst into Fred's office. "We've just got to stop Walt. You know he'd be bad for the city. There must be a way."

"Well, good morning to you, too, Ken."

"I'm sorry. How are you this morning?"

"Fine, fine. I do have a little bit of a development to tell you about."

"Go on. Go on."

"As you know, Joe is the only uncommitted vote out of the seven of us."

"Yeah, but he's still just one vote. Whoever can get his vote will still be one vote short."

"I know. I know. Just hear me out."

"I'm sorry. Tell me your news."

"Joe stopped into my office early this morning and told me he's willing to be the fourth and winning vote for whoever can come to him with three solid votes."

"You're kidding, right? He doesn't like Walt any better than we do. Why would he do that?"

"He thinks we're all qualified and he says it doesn't make any difference. Says the people will decide in the election next year anyway."

"That doesn't make sense. Whoever wins the acting mayor's post will have a chance to prove themselves for a whole year. If they don't screw up too badly, they'll be tough to beat in the election. He should—"

"You and I both know that. I'm just telling you what he said. He seemed to have his mind made up. So if we want to stop Walt, there's only one way to do it. One of us has to drop out and support the other."

Ken was silent for a few seconds before speaking. "You're right. It's the only way, but you know we both want this. So, how do we decide?"

"Let's make this simple. We'll flip a coin."

"Really? We're going to decide something this important on the randomness of a coin toss?"

"Have you got a better idea?"

"I guess not. I'm game. At least we'll get this over with and we can move on—one way or the other. Let's do it, Fred. Wait, let's make this official."

Ken stuck out his hand. "I hereby pledge that if you win the coin toss, I will support you for mayor."

Fred shook his hand and made the same pledge. He then reached into his pants pocket. "Now all we need is a coin and I don't have any change."

Ken reached into his pocket and found a coin. "You call it."

"No, you call it," Fred said.

Ken hesitated as he looked at the coin. "Okay, I call heads, but you toss it."

Fred tossed the coin almost to the ceiling and let it land on the carpet. It was heads.

Chapter Four

"Good morning, Mr. Mayor. Here's your schedule for today. It's a busy one. And your first meeting is already waiting in the lobby."

"Thanks, John. Is everything all set? Can you activate the recording device from your office after you show him in?"

"Yep, we're all set. Just be careful. Remember all the legal advice we got. No entrapment. It all needs to come from him."

"Right, I'm prepared. I'll mostly just listen. Are you as nervous as I am?"

"In a way, yeah. This is serious stuff. Somebody could go to jail over this."

"Well, it won't be me. Be assured I'm gonna do everything above board. We're going to do the right thing—no matter who it is."

As John was leaving the office, he turned back toward the mayor. "Ken, I know this has to be hard. He's been such a long-time supporter and friend."

"Supporter, yes, but he was never really a personal friend. I didn't even know him until I was on the Council. But I do feel a sense of loyalty to him. After all, he was chairman for my last mayoral campaign and he raised about two million dollars. So, yeah, this is hard for me."

"Okay, I'll go get him now. Good luck."

"Thanks, John."

* * *

"Good morning, Ed. Come in. Sit down. How about some coffee?"

"No, thanks. I'm good. Thanks for agreeing to see me on such short notice."

"Well, of course, I would agree to a meeting. I might not be sitting in this chair if wasn't for the help of you and a lot of other people. No one wins elective office all by themselves."

"Thanks, Ken. Shall we get down to business?"

"By all means. I could tell from your phone call yesterday there were things you would be more comfortable discussing in person."

"Very true. I probably said too much in that call as it is."

"Well, I think I got the general gist, but the floor is yours. Go ahead."

"That's one of the things I've always liked about you. For a politician, you're always straight forward. You're not naïve in the ways of the world like so many I have to deal with."

"I suppose, as a developer, you've been forced to deal with a lot of elected officials."

"Yeah, it comes with the territory. But I'm so appreciative that you've always been very pro-development."

"That's a no-brainer. Development, when done right, is good for the city. I've always encouraged cooperation and compromise to get things done."

"You have for sure, but, Ken, your Planning Department is being stubborn on this one and it's a huge project for my company—maybe the biggest development we've ever tackled. It's worth millions, so I promised my partners I could deliver your support."

"Ed, I'm not sure you should have made that promise, but I'm willing to listen. You know I rarely overrule the department. It's only a recommendation anyway and the final decision on all zoning changes is up to the Council. I assume you've lobbied them?"

"Of course, but we just don't have the votes. With some neighbors up in arms and with the department's position, we're in real trouble. I need your help, and I don't expect it to come for free."

The mayor was silent for a few seconds. "Ed, you've earned my support for many projects in the past because I believed they were good projects. They helped the city grow and brought in new sales tax dollars. Wait, what are you saying? What do you mean you don't expect it to come for free?"

"I knew we could be blunt with each other. Listen, I know you've been thinking of running for the U.S. Senate next year. It's an open seat, so you know it'll be very competitive."

"It's true that I've been mulling it over, but I'm really not sure. Suzie and I have talked a lot about it. We're just not sure we want to live in Washington. We love it here. This is our town."

"Ken, many of my friends think you'd make a great senator and you've got what it takes to go even further, maybe the White House. Not everyone is in a position to realize that dream, but *you* are, so you really shouldn't pass up this opportunity."

"Enough about my political future. Let's get back to the zoning issue. I just don't see enough reason to overrule the planners on this one, Ed. I'm really sorry."

"Okay, let me be even *more* blunt. If you give us your support on this one, I'll make sure your Senate campaign will be more than well funded, and you know I can deliver on that promise."

"Wow. I guess I was already counting on your support, but I didn't know it would come with strings attached."

"We're even willing to go an extra step. There are ways—legal ways—you could benefit personally, as well. You could have a stake in one of our other developments. Maybe one that's not so controversial."

"But are you saying that if I don't go along, I've lost your support?"

"Frankly, yes. And a lot of my friends will look for another candidate as well."

Ken rose from his desk chair. "Ed, I'm afraid this meeting is over. I'm not for sale."

"Now, calm down. Don't be so dramatic. You need to think this over. I don't need an answer today."

"Well, you're getting my answer today. The answer is no."

"So, you're telling me that you'd rather be right than be Senator or President, or whatever that saying is?"

"Yes, that's exactly what I'm saying. Good day, Ed."

CHAPTER FIVE

SEVEN MONTHS LATER

From the *Daily Dispatch*

Developer Sentenced to Five Years
In Zoning Bribery Scandal

Ed Owens, long-time local developer, was sentenced Thursday to five years in the state penitentiary and fined $5 million by District Court Judge Robert Howard. He'll be eligible for parole in two and a half years.

Owens was found guilty of attempting to bribe an elected official when he sought support from Mayor Ken Connelly for a zoning change for the proposed Pacific Gateway multi-use development on the northeast side of the city.

Owens stood emotionless as Judge Howard lectured him from the bench. "You were a leader in this community and that means you should be someone setting an example for how business and local government can work together, but you have failed your city, your family and yourself."

Trial testimony, backed up by tape recordings, indicated that Owens offered the mayor a personal interest in a development project, as well as financial support for his upcoming campaign for the U.S. Senate, if he would agree to order the City Planning Department to endorse his project. Mayor Connelly rejected the offers and backed his Planning Department's recommendation against the project.

In an ironic twist, the development was sold to another firm and, after some minor changes to the project, the necessary zoning change received unanimous approval from the City Council. A ground-breaking ceremony is scheduled for next month.

TWO MONTHS LATER

From the *Daily Dispatch*-Editorial Page

Bonus for Voters

In an age where voters have every right to be cynical about elected officials and candidates, the results of Tuesday's U.S. Senate election might be considered a bonus.

Naturally, voters want someone who agrees with them on the issues, but they can't always match that with a candidate who's got character and integrity. With the election of Ken Connelly, they got both. His victory wasn't a total surprise, as Mayor Connelly had unprecedented bi-partisan support for a partisan office, as well as this newspaper's endorsement.

There is little doubt that character was front and center in the hard-fought campaign. The mayor's heroic standing up to one of his biggest supporters seemed to tell voters all they needed to know and with the recent sentencing of developer Ed Owens in the zoning bribery scandal, the issue was fresh on everyone's mind.

Even before that, the two-term mayor had established the reputation of a man who was willing to seek common ground with members of both parties. He never let disagreements, even vehement ones, prevent him from working with those same people on other issues for the good of the city.

This isn't to suggest that Senator-Elect Connelly is a saint. He ran a tough campaign and hit his opponent hard on the issues, but there were no personal attacks, no exaggerating his foe's positions and his TV ads didn't include photos of his opponent looking like a crazy person.

It is our hope that Mr. Connelly will apply these same admirable methods when he gets to the nation's capital.

CHAPTER SIX

Fred was nervous. The arena was cavernous. Banners and balloons filled every empty space. Placards with the names of every state of the union were scattered throughout the convention hall. He had never given a speech in front of a crowd this huge and this raucous, not to mention the millions watching on television.

He straightened his tie and tugged at the bottom of his suit jacket. He strode to the podium with as much confidence as he could muster. The applause was lighter than other speakers had received earlier in the evening.

He looked out at the delegates through his teleprompter and began slowly. "Ladies and gentlemen, I want to thank you for inviting me here tonight, especially since I am not a member of your esteemed party."

A scattering of boos filled the otherwise silent pause. Fred laughed. "I guess I should have expected that."

A lone voice called out, "We're always happy to accept converts."

Fred laughed again and was able to relax through the rest of his speech. As he was nearing the close, he was hitting his stride.

"Ken Connelly has more than proven himself to be a man of integrity. And he has shown that he is willing to work with members of both parties. My standing here tonight is evidence of that.

"He is the rare elected official who can have a strong disagreement with folks on one issue, then look for common ground with those same people on other issues. He proved that when we worked together on the City Council. He did that as Mayor. And he has done that as a United States Senator.

"This country badly needs that in Washington and in the White House.

"In conclusion, I want to share with you a story that tells you something else you ought to know about Ken Connelly. It goes back a lot of years. I saw it with my own eyes. There was a time when this man was willing to give up politics for the sake of his family.

"His becoming mayor wasn't a foregone conclusion. It was a contentious battle and when he and I met one morning, he told me he was ready to give it all up, go back to his business and support me for the position. I knew it was true. I could see it in his eyes. Here was a natural leader who didn't feel he had to be the one. But due to some quirky circumstances—I won't bore you with all of the details—he ended up becoming Mayor and the rest is history. The point is he put principles and family ahead of power.

"And don't you think it's better to have power in the hands of someone who isn't obsessed with getting it or will do anything to obtain it, someone who can walk away from it like Ken Connelly was willing to do so many years ago?

"This man will be a bright light in the White House, a light so bright that it will shine all across this great nation. And that's why I am proud to offer my endorsement for the next president of the United States, Ken Connelly."

The crowd erupted with thunderous applause, whooping and whistling. Rock music blared from the sound system. Fred flushed with pride and waved as he exited the stage.

CHAPTER SEVEN

"**O**f course, I remember the coin toss. How could I forget? It changed both of our lives. But I have no regrets. I've had a great career and I have a great family. I've got five grandkids now. I'm not sure I could have juggled family and politics as well as you have."

"Well, Suzie deserves all the credit, really. She gave up her career to take care of the kids and to take care of me. She made sure they had a normal upbringing and she kept *me* from getting too big of a head."

"Yes, you were blessed to have a great wife."

"Anyway, Fred, come over here. There's something I want to show you."

As they walked over to a glass case in one of the bookcases in the President's inner office, Fred noticed a wall hanging.

And don't you think it's better to have power in the hands of someone who isn't obsessed with getting it or will do anything to obtain it, someone who can walk away from it like Ken Connelly was willing to do so many years ago?

—Fred Otterberg

Those words were displayed in large type inside a simple wooden frame.

"Yeah, Suzie had that done. She thought your speech at that first convention was one of the best in history. She especially liked the part about my willingness to give it all up for the sake of the family. But here, this is what I've been wanting to show you."

Fred was wide-eyed when he saw the coin. "The coin! You saved it. You really saved it. Wow."

"Many people have asked about it, but I never tell them the whole story. I just say that it was given to me by my daughter Janie on the morning before the acting mayor's contest was decided, and that's true, but it's not the *whole* story."

"Janie gave that to you? I don't think I knew that."

"She was showing me a magic trick before I had to rush out the door. Then she handed it to me and said I should keep it for good luck. It came from her magician's kit. It looks like a fifty-cent piece, but it's not a real coin."

The President reached into the glass display case and lifted out the coin. "Fred, I want you to see this for yourself. Here, look at it carefully."

Fred twirled the coin in his fingers. It showed a bust of John F. Kennedy. The words "LIBERTY" formed a half circle at the top and "In God We Trust" spanned the lower part. But when Fred turned the coin to the other side, there was no eagle on the back. It was identical to the Kennedy side. It was a two-headed coin.

Fred's facial expression was unchanged as he handed it back. "Why are you showing me this now?"

"It's bothered me all of these years and I guess I finally wanted to come clean and you're the only person it made sense to tell. It was *you* that I cheated. You didn't have any change in your pockets that day."

"Yeah, I remember. And you said you had one coin."

"I'd forgotten I had it and when I reached in my pocket, it was the only piece I had. I knew it was the coin Janie had given me and I knew it was two-headed. All I had to do was say we needed to go find another coin. I wanted to say it.

"The words were there in my head, but they didn't come out. I held it in my hand for a few seconds before handing it to you to flip it. I cheated and I knew I was doing it. In a way, Fred, those few seconds make my whole career a fraud. I just had to get it off my chest and confess. No one else knows, not even Suzie."

"Ken, your whole career wasn't a fraud. Besides, I sort of knew all along. Not for sure, but I had a pretty good idea."

"Are you serious? You knew and you've supported me all of these years? And that convention speech…" He pointed to the framed quote on the wall.

"Like I said, I wasn't totally sure. I saw the hesitation on your face and I thought the coin felt funny, but I didn't want to look at it too carefully. It would have seemed like I didn't trust you. And besides, there's something I never told you."

"What's that?"

"Before you came in that morning, I had all but decided that I was going to drop out and support you for mayor. Then I came up with the coin toss thing, and I thought it was such a fun idea that I went ahead and suggested it. Even if I'd won the toss, I might have dropped out."

"But Fred, didn't you think less of me for cheating?"

"No one's perfect, Ken, and you more than proved yourself before and after as a man of integrity, so I was willing to overlook it and I have no regrets. Still, I'm glad you told me. But why did you *keep* it all these years? Weren't you afraid someone might see it and figure out the story?"

"I kept it for two reasons. First, it's kept me humble. It was a constant reminder that my goody-two-shoes image wasn't real, so I worked even harder to live up to that reputation."

"And the second reason?"

"It was just a good reminder that life is full of luck, especially in politics. It can turn on a dime, or should I say a fifty-cent piece. Fred, I hadn't planned on doing this, but now that you've told me you knew, I want you to have the coin as a small token of my appreciation for the kind of man who can forgive and overlook another's weaknesses."

Fred took the coin. "Thanks. I'll cherish this, Mr. President."

The End

THE
BIRTHDAY

CHAPTER ONE
THE PARTY

George sat at the head of the table, beaming. He was all spiffed up, wearing a sport coat and tie. All the people he loved were there: his sons Ken and Marty, his daughter Caroline, their spouses, and all five of George's grandkids, ranging in age from thirty to forty-one.

And nine great-grandchildren. Sally, the oldest at fifteen was George's favorite. The youngest, Joey, was six.

One, of course, was missing: Mary Beth, his wife of forty-two years. She'd been gone for twenty-six years, but there wasn't a day he didn't think of her.

But this was a happy day. Any time he had his family around him was a happy day. And the folks at Peaceful Meadows Senior Living, where he had lived for the past ten years, had gone out of their way to make it special, converting the private dining room into a festive party room.

There were streamers galore and a large banner dominated the room. It read, "Happy 90th, George.

We all love you." It was signed by every member of the staff.

Sally stood by the door and watched Great-Aunt Caroline carry a three-layer chocolate cake with white frosting and filled with burning candles. "Okay, everybody, here she comes. I'm going to turn out the lights. Get ready to sing."

The cake was placed in front of George, and after a rousing round of *Happy Birthday*, George paused. He didn't want this moment to end. But after a few seconds, he drew a deep breath and blew as hard as he could.

"Well, I got most of them. Thank God there weren't ninety of 'em."

Everyone clapped and Sally yelled, "We love you, Grandpa."

Joey chimed in, "Yeah, we love you, Gramps." George laughed and the whole group clapped again.

George looked down the table. "Thanks, Mike, I'm glad I don't have shy grandkids—I mean great-grandkids."

"Grandpa, it was me, Joey."

"Oh, of course, Joey. I am so sorry."

As they all ate cake and chatted, George was lost in his thoughts.

Damn, I hate when I get mixed up. I know the difference between Mike and Joey. Sometimes, I just don't know why certain things come out of my mouth. I know they all understand, but it's still so frustrating.

I guess that's what happens when you live this long. Life just isn't going to be perfect. I guess life is never perfect at any age. And I've been okay with that up until now, but I know I'm getting much worse. Sometimes I don't even know where I am or why I'm here.

I think I've made the right decision, but I know it's going to be hard on all of them, especially Sally.

As hard as this is going to be, I'm glad I chucked the pill idea. It would have been too sudden and it would have meant lying to my doctor in order to store up enough sleeping pills. This is definitely the better way.

I can barely get around, even with my walker. I know I'm getting weaker by the day. I've fallen several times lately and I know it's only a matter of time before I break a hip and…

But maybe the worst thing is waking up in the morning and realizing I've wet my bed. I start most days angry and frustrated with myself. I know I'm becoming more and more of a burden to everyone. And wearing these—I don't care what they're called. They're still diapers. It's humiliating.

Then there're times when I feel like I'm in a dream, even though I know I'm awake. Everything is all jumbled up in my head and nothing makes sense. That's when I just go all quiet if anyone's around. I know they wonder what's going on, but I just don't want to embarrass myself.

And most days I'm bored out of my mind. I can't track what's going on in a TV program or even a baseball game. The days are long and I feel like I'm just sitting around waiting to die.

"Grandpa, you're not eating your cake," shouted Joey.

"Yes, I am. I've had two bites. My appetite isn't what it used to be."

"That's okay, Dad. Just eat what you want," Caroline said.

"Thanks, sweetheart. I am so blessed to have you all here and on such a beautiful fall day."

"Gramps, it's June," Joey said. "You're birthday's in June."

"June. Of course, it's June. It's hot out there, I bet."

"Yeah, it's going to be ninety, same as you, Gramps."

Everyone laughed.

George pushed his plateful of cake off to the side and reached into the inside pocket of his sport coat and pulled out three envelopes.

"I hate to put a damper on this wonderful occasion, but I have something I want to talk to you all about. And since I wasn't sure I could get through it without being overcome by emotion or confusion, I've written a letter I would like you all to read. The staff has reserved a nearby room with a conference table so you can read them in private, talk about it, then come back and we can talk."

All of the adults fidgeted in their seats. "What about the little ones?" Ken asked.

"Let's have the great-grandkids stay here with me for a few minutes, then they can go outside to play when you come back."

Sally stood and put her hands on her hips. "I'm not a kid. I want to be with the adults."

George gazed at her. "You're right, Sal. You go with the adults."

"I see you have three envelopes, though, Dad," Caroline said.

"Yes, but only one is from me. It will all become clear. So off with you. Maybe I'll have a few more bites of cake while you're gone. Take your time. I'm not going anywhere."

CHAPTER TWO
THE LETTERS

To My Beloved Children and
Grandchildren,

I have been so fortunate to have been born
in a time and place where I have been able to
write the script of my own life. I have always
wanted to have a plan, set goals and try to
control as much as possible.

I've always known, of course, that there
are many things that can't be controlled.
Losing Mary Beth after forty-two wonderful
years of marriage certainly brought that
point home to me in a very profound way.

Nonetheless, I've been blessed to have
accomplished much of what I set out to do.
And I've been even more blessed to have all of
you as the most important people in my life.
You know how much I love all of you.

Recently, as you know, I've been diagnosed
with Alzheimer's. Naturally, I'm not happy
about it, but I must accept it. We're all going

to die of something. The biggest downside, however, is that, in losing my mental faculties, I will no longer be able to continue to make my own rational decisions. Having enjoyed the freedoms I've enjoyed all of my life, this is something I can not accept.

With that in mind, and having reached the ripe old age of ninety, and before it's too late, I would like to be able to write the ending to that script. So I have made the decision to shorten my life by fasting.

As you will see from the letter from my doctor, I have been authorized to enter a hospice facility, where I will be well cared for until the end. I will not be suffering and the end should come within a few weeks at the most.

In the big scheme of things, it doesn't really matter whether I die at age ninety or ninety-two, ninety-six, or one hundred. It's been a great life, and I would not like my last years to be spent in dark confusion, not to mention becoming a tremendous burden to those around me.

I know. I know. I can already hear you saying I wouldn't be a burden, but we all know that's not true.

I want to go out with my heart and mind full of love from all of you and I want you to remember me the way I am. Well, maybe not this old, but still, you know what I mean.

When you finish reading this, I am open to discussing it and to answering your questions, *but I hope you will come to understand and respect my decision.*

I also have letters from my physician and my attorney, which you might find helpful and reassuring.

Let me say again how much I love you all.

Love,
Dad/Grandpa

FROM THE OFFICE OF SAMUEL D. GROSS. M.D.

To the Family of George Rooney:

George Rooney has been my patient for nearly twenty years. Over that time, he has become more than just a patient. I consider him a true friend, and I have nothing but the utmost respect for him, the way his mind works, and the sound decisions he has made throughout his life.

Sadly, he was recently diagnosed with Alzheimer's. That is a progressive disease and is not curable. The speed of the disease and how quickly it might severely diminish a person's memory and ability to think clearly is unpredictable. When the onset occurs at older ages, such as in George's case, the time tends to be much shorter.

Because of this, George has chosen not to wait, but rather to shorten his time left by fasting. When he came to me to discuss this, I did not try to convince him one way or the other, but I did spend a lot of time going over with him all the ramifications to be sure he was making this decision with all of the facts at his disposal.

I am convinced he is of sound mind and making this decision out of love for his family and a sincere desire to exercise his free choice, while it is still possible.

I have, therefore, arranged and authorized him to become a patient at the Sarah Williams Hospice House here in town. There he will be well cared for and kept comfortable and pain-free.

I would be happy to meet with any family members if you would wish to discuss this further.

Sincerely,
Sam Gross, M.D.

From the Law Offices of Jack Watson, Attorney at Law

To Whom it May Concern:

I am writing this on behalf of my client, George Rooney.

As you know by now, he has made the decision to shorten his life through fasting and it is his intention to enter a hospice facility for the last days of his life.

He is of sound mind and has the legal right to make this decision.

Although he already has a living will, his decision, as stated in his letter to you, supersedes that document and should legally be considered his final wishes. He has not made any changes to his legal will.

I want to reassure you that his actions and that of the hospice house in accepting him are completely within the laws of our state and that any assistance, care, comfort, and support you may offer will not constitute any illegal actions.

At the facility, he will be offered food and water, but it is his intention to only accept water. He understands he can change his mind and rescind his letter of intention and leave the hospice facility at any time.

If you have any questions, please feel free to give me a call.

Jack Watson
Attorney at Law

Chapter Three
THE DEBATE

Caroline blinked back tears. "But, Dad, you're doing okay. There's no cancer, and you only take a few meds for high blood pressure."

"Doing okay? You're kidding, right? It's painful shuffling from place to place, only to sit in my chair and sleep. Call them Depends or whatever. I call them diapers. And I can't always tell the difference between a fart and something more. Sweetheart, I'm confused much of the time, and it's getting more frequent. I have moments of clarity, sure, but more and more, it's the other way. I need to do this before it's too late and I'm confused one hundred percent of the time."

As the discussion continued, Sally calmly rose from her chair, strolled over to George and put her arms around him and hugged hard.

George turned toward her and kissed her cheek. "Such a sweet girl."

"But Grandpa, I'll miss you too much. I love you so much. Please, don't do this."

"I knew it would be the hardest for you. But it would be hard whether it's now or five years from now."

Through her tears, Sally shouted. "But won't you miss *us,* Grandpa?"

"Well, I would, except I won't know I'm missing you. I'll be gone."

"Don't you care about us?" As her crying increased, she ran from the room.

She returned a few minutes later. "I'm sorry, Grandpa. I know you love us. I'm being immature. I'll try to be grown-up about this."

George smiled silently and they hugged.

Marty, who had been silent during the discussions, rose from his chair as if he had been called upon to give a speech. He paused and looked around the room at his siblings and his nieces and nephews.

"Dad, I for one will respect your decision. But to make this easier on all of us, will you agree to think it over a little longer before you make your final decision? It's a lot for us to take in. Maybe Caroline, Ken and I could meet with you privately in the next day or so."

"Sure, I'm open to talking more. I'm not scheduled to be admitted to the hospice house for another couple of weeks. Thanks, Marty, for your support. It means a lot to me. Now let's have that ice cream."

Chapter Four
HOSPICE HOUSE

The nurse walked into George's room to check on him. Seeing that his head had slipped off his pillow, she re-adjusted it for him.

He opened his eyes. "Thank you, nurse. I'm sorry I can't remember your name."

"It's Becky, but that's okay George. I'm amazed how you're always so grateful for even the little things we do for you."

George opened his eyes a little wider. "Well, even if I did want to complain, you're way too nice and way too pretty."

She blushed. "You're a kind man. I'll bet you were quite a hit with the ladies in your day."

"Not really. Just one lady, my dear Mary Beth."

Becky smiled and George smiled back weakly. "I may be old and I may be dying, but I can still see."

"Okay, George, I've got to go now, but I'll be back later to check on you."

George closed his eyes and fell asleep.

* * *

Sally thought it was strange that the place seemed so cheery. The walls were painted different colors, but all bright: yellow, turquoise, orange. Thick carpets and low ceilings created a tranquil ambiance. Soft, but uplifting music filled the hallway as she walked toward George's room.

When she came to the door, she saw he was asleep. There was an IV attached to his arm.

One of the staff nurses saw her standing at the door. "It's okay; you can go in."

"But he looks so peaceful."

"Yes, he sleeps most of the time now, but you can wake him. Here, I'll do it for you. He'll want to see you."

She gently touched his arm. "George, one of your granddaughters is here to see you. Can you wake up for a few minutes?"

George's eye flickered open, then closed again, then open. He smiled.

"Grandpa, it's me, Sally."

"Sally, you're looking as beautiful as ever. Thanks for coming to see me."

"Grandpa, I'm amazed you have such a nice smile on your face."

"Well, there are two reasons for that. I'm smiling because it's the way I want you to remember me, and I'm smiling because I've had such a great life."

After a short time, George's eyes began to close, and Sally wasn't sure if she should stay. She stepped out in the hall and saw the nurse who had helped her before.

"He fell back asleep."

"It's okay. He's on pretty heavy meds to make sure he's not in pain. He's getting very weak. But he knows you were here. You can stay a little longer if you'd like."

"No, I think I'll go, but thanks for your help."

Epilogue

From the *High Plains News-Gazette*

Former Newspaper
Publisher Dies at 90

George. M. Rooney, the long-time editor-publisher of the *High Plains News-Gazette*, died Tuesday at age 90.

Rooney was born in Indian Point, Nebraska April 1, 1930. He graduated from the University of Nebraska School of Journalism and served in the Marine Corps during the Korean War.

He married Mary Beth O'Brien in 1952. He worked at newspapers in Shenandoah, Iowa and Lincoln, Nebraska before buying this paper in 1960. His wife was the advertising manager until her death in 1994.

"Mr. Rooney had the reputation of a hard-hitting journalist who wouldn't back down from a good story even when it occasionally cost him some advertising revenue," said Cal Smith, the current editor.

"He was a respected member of this community for more than forty years," according to Sid Weaver, president of the Chamber of Commerce. "He will be missed."

Rooney sold the newspaper in 1995 and started a small print shop, which he ran for another ten years before retiring at age 75. He was most recently living at Peaceful Meadows Senior Living. He passed away at the Sarah Williams Hospice House.

Services are pending. Rooney is survived by two sons, Ken and Marty Rooney, one daughter, Caroline Larson and five grandchildren.

The End

ABOUT THE AUTHOR

The author lives in Green Valley, Arizona.
Comments welcome at jimcleary72@gmail.com

OTHER BOOKS BY JIM CLEARY

Prisoner in Paradise

A unique combination of adventure, romance and fantasy.

Propelled in a heartbeat from a war zone to being captive in a picturesque mountain forest, journalist Sean O'Donnell knows he won't be going home to his beautiful wife any time soon. But when other captives appear, will he want to?

And how long will the woman he left behind wait for her missing husband before having him declared dead and moving on with her life?

Not knowing the identify of his captors is only one of the hurdles he must overcome to gain his freedom, but his fellow captives may pose an even bigger barrier.

Prisoner in Paradise is an unusual survival tale, filled with romantic entanglements and plot twists.

SONG CREDITS

Jessie's Girl
1981
Composer: Rick Springfield
Popular Recording: Rick Springfield

We Gotta Get Out of This Place
1965
Composers: Barry Mann and Cynthia Weil
Popular Recording: The Animals

SPECIAL THANKS TO

Quindrid Godden, my dear wife, who was invaluable as a first reader and editor and who made dozens of suggestions to help improve the stories. Thanks, too, for her love and encouragement.

Early readers: Bonnie Papenfuss and Joy Schulz
Chris O'Byrne for the final edit.
Debbie O'Byrne for the cover design.

Made in the USA
Columbia, SC
14 June 2021